THE HIDE AND SEEK CORPSE

THE HIDE AND SEEK CORPSE

Jane McLoughlin

CHIVERS
THORNDIKE

This Large Print book is published by BBC Audiobooks Ltd, Bath, England and by Thorndike Press®, Waterville, Maine, USA.

Published in 2005 in the U.K. by arrangement with Robert Hale Ltd.

Published in 2005 in the U.S. by arrangement with Robert Hale Limited.

U.K. Hardcover ISBN 1–4056–3338–7 (Chivers Large Print)
U.K. Softcover ISBN 1–4056–3339–5 (Camden Large Print)
U.S. Softcover ISBN 0–7862–7578–2 (Buckinghams)

The text of this Large Print edition is unabridged.
Other aspects of the book may vary from the original edition.

Set in 16 pt. New Times Roman.

Printed in Great Britain on acid-free paper.

British Library Cataloguing in Publication Data available

Library of Congress Cataloging-in-Publication Data

McLoughlin, Jane.
The hide and seek corpse / Jane McLoughlin.
p. cm.
ISBN 0–7862–7578–2 (lg. print : sc : alk. paper)
1. Women detectives—England—Fiction. 2. Capitalists and financiers—Fiction. 3. Corporations—Fiction. 4. England—Fiction. 5. Large type books. I. Title.
PR6063.C573H53 2005
823'.914—dc22 2005002606

CHAPTER ONE

The weekend that Fanny Dinmont found the dead body started much the same as any other, with Fanny battling the traffic and thinking that whoever said it was better to travel hopefully than to arrive had never had to join the Friday night stampede of weekenders leaving London for the country.

But Rowfield isn't very far from London and she'd arrived before she really had time to dwell on the thought that it was a shame how such a good-looking, sexy young woman was spending another weekend alone. Time enough for that later when she was lying in bed when it would undoubtedly cross her mind that she was going to waste.

Fanny leaned her head back against the car seat and listened to the sudden silence after she turned off the engine. Gradually she began to hear the small friendly familiar sounds, the faint moan of The Black Bull Inn sign swinging in the breeze, the rustle of a nocturnal animal in the dry grass under the hedge, the faint protest of sleepy birds disturbed by her arrival. Fanny smiled. The magic had worked again. The car was a time machine. She took off in her capsule on Fridays from a seething, noisy London street, drove fifty miles in a constant stream of crawling traffic, and emerged in a different, unrelated, world.

Tall, slim and dark-haired, with a full mouth and a long straight nose that gave her an intelligent look, she got out of the car and stretched. She was tall enough to find her old Renault a tight fit. She leaned into the back seat and pulled out her weekend bag—Kafka, this week's *Economist* magazine, four pairs of clean knickers, men's pyjamas to sleep in and a sexy black satin peignoir just in case. When she'd been married to Alan, she'd have brought walking shoes, provisions and Jane Austen, but she was divorced now, even if she was still half in love with her husband, which was ridiculous because he had married again.

I'm pathetic, she said to herself. The Kafka was pathetic, improving her mind with intellectual novels. The *Economist* as well.

'What do I really know about business?' she said aloud. The sexy black peignoir, too. Who did she think she was going to meet in the village to wear that for?

The bar of The Black Bull, a genuine old coaching inn, was closed, the car-park almost empty. A great big beautiful harvest moon came out for a moment from behind a cloud. It lit up The Bull's grounds and the gate in the low fence which led into the garden of Fanny's cottage. She swore, as she did most Friday nights, as her high-heeled shoes sank into the grass. This path from The Bull's grounds where she was allowed to leave her car was much shorter than walking round through the village and down the path to the front door of her cottage, but on early autumn nights like this the grass was always wet. The shoes were thin, interview shoes, London shoes, drenched in the heavy cold dew.

It was the same every week, but every week she came through the garden. Coming on the cottage this way, she had the feeling that the place had been waiting just for her. It was like coming home to an old dog. It wasn't the same walking round the front, past the row of thatched cottages down the narrow path, with the scent of honeysuckle still heavy in the air under the curtained windows of her sleeping neighbours. That reminded her that she was not part of daily life here, she was the weekender, the frivolous taster of the village. She knew the locals laughed at her, with her London hair and her silly shoes; at her cottage too, with the sliding glass door on to the garden at the back, and the open-plan downstairs room and the spiral staircase leading to the platform landing upstairs. Fanny had not herself made these unprecedented innovations in the sixteenth-century terrace of otherwise identical cottages, but as far as the villagers were concerned she might as well have done.

She opened the sliding glass door and stepped into the sitting-room. The room struck cold, a little damp. She dropped her weekend bag and picked her way carefully to the light switch by the fireplace, feeling the familiar arm of the settee and the sharp edge of the coffee table. She tripped over the carpet, her new prize, a glowing strip woven with the colours of jewels which she had put down the week before. It was old, in parts threadbare, the edge frayed, but like walking on stained glass. She moved carefully so as not to trip again.

She switched on the lights, blinking. She shivered. The night behind the glass door she had left partly open reflected *a film noir* version of the room, cold and mysterious. She wouldn't bother with a fire, just turn on the heating, put on the kettle, and perhaps watch television in bed. It would take hours for the cottage to warm up.

She turned back to close the door.

When she saw the body she did not scream. She gasped at the shock, but that was all. She felt blood surging this way and that, hot inside her cold skin.

Her first reaction was to turn off the lights.

In the sudden blackness she stood quite still, listening. If there was someone in the house, he would surely give himself away, some small noise, a creaking floorboard, the sound of breathing. He would surely come out from his hiding place to see what she was doing in the silence.

There was nothing. No sound at all.

Fanny was used to the groans and creaks and mutterings of an old house but they were still now.

She put on the lights again. Trying not to look as she stepped past the battered head of the body, she shut the glass door and closed the curtains. If there was someone out there, she did not want him watching her.

The body sprawled across the rich colours of her carpet was as discreet as such a thing can be. The corpse wore a neat grey suit, legs tucked under the coffee table, dark socks unwrinkled. Fanny expected his expression to be one of apology for troubling her, like an unpractised drunk after throwing up.

She looked at his face and rushed to the kitchen, retching into the sink. She turned on the cold tap, then swallowed handfuls of cold water, slapping it on her face and neck.

She knew him. He was not a stranger. He was someone she had met. That very day, in fact. That made it worse. His body was not on her living-room floor by chance, but for some reason. It was too much of a coincidence otherwise.

To say she knew him was going too far. She knew who he was. She'd talked to him for a few minutes, not much more. They'd chatted in the outer office of TROD headquarters in the City that morning while his boss finished a long distance telephone call before interviewing her. He'd still been there later when she left, and she'd told him she'd got the job as the new public relations consultant. He'd smiled and said they'd be seeing more of each other then. He'd obviously read the resume of her career she'd sent in with her letter of application, because he'd made some dry little joke about her being a poacher turned gamekeeper, going into public relations after being a freelance journalist, and she'd thought that was kind of him because she'd never been enough of a journalist to earn a proper living if she hadn't been married to Alan. And she'd wanted to say that really getting the job wasn't altogether a reason for celebrating either, because there was something pathetic about your ex-husband getting you a job.

But she hadn't said anything because he seemed genuinely pleased for her, and she didn't want to spoil his pleasure. It had occurred to her at the time, she remembered, that he looked as though he could do with any little bit of pleasure he could get out of life. He'd seemed to her to be the absolute epitome of a man whose whole life had been a succession of identical days where nothing much happened at all. Try as she might, she could think of nothing to suggest he was anything more than a hard-working and meticulous personal assistant to Sir Stafford Williams, the head of the convoluted corporate body where she had won the task of putting a friendly public face on the company's broad and sometimes mysterious international interests.

Now he lay with his skull bashed in among the rich colours of her living-room rug.

Fanny knelt and touched him. He was not cold. The blood was still wet in the wound on his head. His eyes stared up at her. She could not even remember what Sir Stafford had called him in that crisp little voice of his. Bellow, was it? Buckle? Some name like that. She remembered thinking it suited him, like a butler in P.G. Wodehouse.

She stood up and turned away. She must telephone the police, but there was no phone in the cottage and she'd left her mobile in London. She did that to avoid fretting because she had no one to call her. And at the cottage she'd got tired of answering calls for Alan after he left, having to explain why she couldn't take a message. She'd had it cut off, and hadn't missed it until now. She reached for her handbag to find coins, then remembered you don't need coins to call the police in an emergency. She crept across the room to the front door, flung it open, and rushed into the lane.

It was dark in the village street, and quiet. People went to bed early here, and the pubs were long closed. Her heels sounded like gunfire on the cobbled pavement as she ran into the High Street. Surely someone must wake and wonder who was running like this so late. But no light came on in a bedroom; even curiosity did not ruffle the placid calm of the sleeping village.

The telephone box was tucked behind the bridge across the river which surrounded the village on three sides. As she hurried round the twist in the road past The Black Bull, with its creaking sign, she could see the light in the kiosk. Inside she made out, in the glow of the dim bulb, the dark form of someone using it.

A man, a very tall thin man, was hunched over the receiver as though he was having trouble making himself heard. Fanny knew who he was. She had seen him in the bar at The Bull, the mysterious, good-looking American who had come to house-sit the old Manor House behind the church. People in the pub talked about him. He was a cartoonist, who apparently worked into the night and seldom appeared by day. Usually alone, but visitors came after dark, glimpsed against uncurtained windows, or in the flash of light as the front door opened. The man who owned the old Manor was a newcomer, and the village had made a mystery out of him. Now that he had gone away somewhere and the American had come to live there, the people in the village transferred their suspicions to him. Fanny had heard some of the stories, that he was a spy, that he made blue movies, that he was an international drugs baron, fabulously wealthy.

Fanny had seen him walking by the river in the late evening, after the families and the cheerful hikers had long gone home. A tall dark handsome man in tweeds who looked as though he smelled of pipe smoke, wearing a battered hat, striding along with his eyes on the ground, apparently unaware of the two ecstatic little grey terriers which wrestled and raced around his feet. He was dog-sitting as well as looking after the house.

Now this handsome American showed no sign of ending his conversation. She stamped and coughed outside the kiosk, shivering in her thin blouse. He was oblivious. She thought of the dead man growing stiff on her carpet and banged on the glass.

She saw him see her. He frowned and shook his head, not breaking his concentration on what was being said to him. She banged again and mouthed at him, 'Help! Police!' With an exasperated gesture he put his hand over the receiver and pushed the door open with his foot.

'Say, can't you wait your turn?'

'Murder! There's been a murder. In my house. There's a body on my sitting-room floor.'

She could hear her voice rising hysterically, and took a deep breath.

'I've got to call the police,' she said.

'You don't say,' he said, watching her as though he were trying to decide if this was some female ploy to get him off the line. 'OK,' he said.

He let the door bang shut, said something sharply into the receiver and hung up. Then he came out, holding the door open for her.

She tried to dial, but her fingers slipped and fumbled. He had not shut the door, leaning over her curiously. He pushed her shaking hand away and dialled 999. The number began to ring, and he nodded at her and backed out of the box.

Fanny surprised herself by telling the police what had happened in a cold, businesslike way which sounded rehearsed until she realized she was copying the manner of a thousand TV crime dramas.

The sergeant calmly asked questions. She answered him with equal detachment.

Finally he said, 'Go home and wait. We'll be as quick as we can.'

She listened to the dialling tone. Her legs felt weak. Her wet feet felt very cold. The door of the telephone box was heavy as she pushed it open.

She walked slowly away towards the High Street, then stopped. She didn't want to wait in the cottage for the police to come. She wandered towards the river which flowed under the road to her right and leaned over the parapet of the bridge looking down into the water. The current was strong and the fast-moving water caught the light from the telephone box. Beyond its range, though, she could see nothing. But the sound it made was reassuring.

At last she turned to go home. The police would be there soon. She walked briskly away towards the silent houses of the High Street.

Then she jumped and almost screamed as a man stepped out of the shadows in front of her. It was the handsome American.

'My God!' she said. 'You startled me.'

'I'm sorry,' he said. 'I hung around because I thought you might be able to use some help.'

He's waited for me, she thought. That was nice of him. And she'd been ages on the bridge. She wished she could remember his name. She'd heard it often enough. It was something unlikely, as if he'd made it up.

'They're on their way, right?' he said. 'Come on. It won't take them long this time of night.'

He took her elbow.

'Where do you live?' he asked.

'Down Hop Lane,' she said.

'Oh, it's real pretty down there. Real traditional, with the thatch, and those little bedroom windows at head level under the eaves.'

'They're bigger inside than they look. You step down from the front door.'

He still had hold of her elbow and was half pushing her along. She struggled to keep up with him.

'When were they built?' he asked. 'They look ancient.'

'They are,' she said. 'I think the original structure is medieval, but mostly they're sixteenth century.'

'You don't say,' he said. He sounded impressed.

Fanny began to laugh.

'For heaven's sake,' she said, 'there's a man lying dead on my floor and we talk like guests at a cocktail party.'

Fanny's smile wobbled. She was afraid she was going to cry. That poor old man, and they were making jokes.

They had reached the turn into the lane. Fanny stopped.

'Thanks,' she said, 'I'll be fine now.'

'Do you think I'd leave you to go home on your own? That would be a breach of etiquette, and I could do with that drink you're about to offer me.'

Fanny shrugged. Clearly he didn't altogether believe her, even though he'd dialled 999 himself. He'd never seemed surprised at her story. Did he think it was an elaborate way of introduction? Or perhaps that she was just plain mad? Well, whatever he thought, she didn't want to sit alone with the dead man waiting for the police.

He was watching her. He smiled.

'I'll never make you English out. You look

as though you're wondering what Miss Manners would say you should do. I mean, how does one behave in the circumstances? Does one make polite conversation as though there wasn't a body on one's carpet? Perhaps if one ignores it, it will go away. Or should one bring it out into the open and discuss it? It's a dilemma, one of the most awkward social occasions one may have to face.'

'Miss Manners isn't English,' Fanny said. 'And she certainly wouldn't approve of me offering you a drink in my own place before we've been introduced. I don't think she'd accept a corpse as chaperon. You should be grateful we're in England, where we're all so terribly improper these days. My name is Fanny Dinmont, by the way. And this is my humble home.'

She opened the front door of the cottage and turned on the light in the tiny lobby so he could see the three steps down inside. She stood back to let him in, as there was no room for them both to pass. He bowed mockingly.

'Gaylord Poyntz at your service, ma'am. Now that etiquette is satisfied, we can cut to the chase. Or rather the chaser. What about that drink?'

'What an extraordinary name! Did you make it up?'

'No, ma'am. My mother did. Well, Miss Dinmont, where's the body? You may not believe this, but this is my first English weekend murder.'

Fanny pointed towards the back of the sitting-room, up one shallow step from the dining area where they were standing. The carpet was hidden by the settee.

'It's there,' she said.

She walked with him towards it. Then she cried out and clutched his hand. 'Oh, my God!'

'There's nothing there,' he said. 'I do think your dustmen are wonderful.'

'It was there. There was a big patterned rug on top of the fitted carpet and the body was on it. It was. I saw it. And I knew him, too.'

This surprised him.

'You knew him?'

'Well, I'd met him. Today as a matter of fact. He was my new boss's right-hand man.'

'You're sure he was dead? Could he have fallen and hit his head and been knocked unconscious? He could've come round and staggered off into the night.'

'Carrying my carpet with him, I suppose? He may have been neat, but that's going a bit far don't you think?' She sat down suddenly on the settee.

'Of course he was dead. And anyway why should he be here in my cottage falling down and hitting his head?'

'Well, you don't have a phone, he could hardly call to say he was coming.'

Fanny was defensive. 'You don't seem to be on the telephone either,' she said.

'For the record, I used the public box to report mine out of order. Now you get us a drink, why don't you, and then we should sit down and figure out what to do about this. Before the police burst in and arrest you.'

'Why should they arrest me?' Fanny asked. 'I haven't done anything.'

'That's what they all say,' Gaylord Poyntz said.

Fanny felt his eyes appraising her. She could see he liked what he saw, and she blushed.

He said, 'They'll arrest you for wasting police time. Your average country cop isn't going to pass up a chance of closer acquaintance with a girl with your looks.'

'I'll get us a drink,' she said.

'Ah,' he said, 'looks *and* intelligence.'

'This isn't a joke. There was a body.'

She went to the screened-off kitchen behind the spiral staircase for glasses and a bottle of Scotch.

Gaylord Poyntz was on his hands and knees on the mushroom carpet. The place where the coloured rug had been showed as a lighter patch on the beige.

He sat back on his heels and drained the glass she handed him, holding it out towards the bottle for a refill.

'It's good for shock,' he said. 'A dead body is a shock. Even being told about it at second-hand is a shock. There's nothing here I can see. Ask me how I can tell you're not a very enthusiastic housewife, Watson.'

'Oh shut up, for God's sake. This is serious. What can I say to the police?'

'We should stick to what's believable. I'll tell them you're a hallucinating lunatic who escaped from my custody, but I'm taking you back to the asylum and we won't let you out on a compassionate visit ever again. Or I'll offer them a sweetener to go away and forget it.'

'Don't be ridiculous. The body *was* here. That poor old man was murdered.'

Gaylord looked doubtful, but he nodded. 'OK, say you're right. How would anyone get the body out? Rolled in the carpet, right?'

'Could one man do that?'

He shrugged.

'Can they get out the back? Is there another way out?'

'Yes, through the glass door. There's a gate to the hotel car park at the bottom of the garden. That's the way I came in. Look.'

She drew back the curtain and turned on a switch which flooded the lawn with light. The fence and the garden gate stood out against the black night beyond.

'Of course the light wasn't on when I came in,' she said.

'One pair of footprints coming this way,' Gaylord said. 'Made by female person of above average height or a man in dancing pumps, one hundred and twenty-five pounds hurrying—certainly not someone weighed down or dragging a body backwards. So he didn't go that way.'

'So he did go out the front,' she said.

They both looked towards the front door where the unshaded light in the lobby glared.

'More likely they, I'd say,' Gaylord said.

'It's a Yale lock. I may have left it open when I went to phone. I can't remember. I did rather rush out in a panic.'

Gaylord picked up the bottle of Scotch from the coffee table and filled his glass. Then he poured some into hers.

'Could they have been hiding in the house when you came in?' he asked.

She shook her head and explained how she had put out the lights and listened.

'I didn't search the place,' she said, 'but I'd have thought there'd have been something, some sound. But there wasn't. And then I rushed out.'

'Impeccable thinking, my dear Fanny,' he said. 'I'd have rushed out too. After I'd regained consciousness.'

'Anyway, you know how houses feel when you're alone in them? I'm sure I'd have felt someone there.'

'Someone *alive*, you mean?'

Fanny said nothing. The silence of the house settled around them. Then she said, 'They could have gone out the back on to the patio and then round the side. There's a path at the side of the house. The oil man uses it when he delivers. There's a gate to the lane.'

Gaylord Poyntz got to his feet.

'Is it locked?' he asked. 'Or do you keep it bolted?'

He slid back the glass door and strode out on to the paved area outside.

'I don't know,' Fanny said, following him. 'I never use it.'

He disappeared into the darkness.

Am I mad? she thought, I don't know anything about Gaylord Poyntz, except that he's American and handsome. He's probably a raving lunatic.

She wondered if he had decided to call it a night and leave her to it. Then he spoke from close beside her in the dark. She jumped. She hadn't heard him coming.

'It's not bolted now,' he said, 'but there's no sign of anything. Not that I could see much. My matches kept going out. Where does the lane go?'

'You're the one who lives here,' she said, 'haven't you ever walked round the village?'

'You will insist on making a tourist out of me. It was a rhetorical question, part of the deductive process, Watson. The lane goes down to the village ring road, right? A single-track dirt road past the allotments where a man commissioned to dispose of a body wrapped in an old carpet could leave his means of transport, correct?'

'No one would be likely to see him, that's

true. There's only the Faulkners and a millionaire's cottage further down the lane. There's never anyone about at night. The millionaire's always getting burgled, except he hardly ever comes here to find out. And the Faulkners are in bed by ten every night. I know, because they've complained about the noise I make "into the small hours" when I put the ten o'clock news on when I get down here on a Friday night.'

She led him back into the cottage. He helped himself to a drink. 'The point is,' he said, 'we know they took a body away from here . . .'

'. . . and a carpet . . .'

'. . . a body and a carpet. But the police, who at this moment are probably speeding across the bridge with their sirens going to clear the empty streets, are not going to believe there ever was a body. Or a carpet, for that matter.'

He smiled. He's got a nice smile, she thought, and he's nice and tall. He had to bend down a little to touch her glass with his in a mocking toast. She wondered why there seemed to be no sign of a Mrs Poyntz, official or unofficial. He must be divorced, she told herself, most Americans seemed to be divorced while they were still in their thirties.

'Sister,' he said, 'you sure as hell better find some story to explain all this.'

There was a heavy knocking at the front door.

'They're here,' she said.

'How do you do it, Holmes?' he asked.

Fanny took a deep breath and went to open the door.

CHAPTER TWO

There were three of them. They rushed through the door as though they had just kicked it down. The last of them missed the steps and fell forward into the others, who stood as though surprised that they had not been met with a burst of gunfire.

'Miss Dimman? I'm D.I. Fulwell.'

He was a large, red-faced man. There was something in his expression which made him look as though nothing in his life had ever impressed him and he didn't intend to let anything minor members of the public might do change that. He pointed at his companions. One was stocky with feet so small that Fanny wondered that they found regulation boots to fit him, the other was a pale-faced uniformed constable with pimples and a constant eager but uneasy smile.

'Kerslake and Mimms,' Inspector Fulwell said, and added, 'Sergeant and Constable.'

Fanny nodded. She wished that she had not heard Gaylord Poyntz laugh over the rural policemen's entrance or their names like a

Jermyn Street shirtmaker.

'Dinmont, actually,' she said.

Inspector Fulwell did not acknowledge the correction of her name. He stood waiting.

Fanny took a deep breath. Then she explained. Watching the inspector as she spoke, she saw that Gaylord was right. She could see it crossing the inspector's mind that she was mad. Then she could see him deciding that she was guilty. Of what she was guilty he didn't know, but whatever it was, she was guilty, he could tell.

'I see,' he said when she finished. 'You say you knew the body previously?'

'I said I knew who he was. I didn't *know* him. I'm not sure of his name. I think it was Burroughs or Barrow, something like that. It began with a B, anyway. He worked for Sir Stafford Williams. You know who I mean? Sir Stafford Williams, the head of TROD?'

'TROD, Miss?'

The three policemen looked at Fanny as though she had started to speak in tongues.

'You must have heard of it. It's always in the newspapers.'

It occurred to Fanny that policemen probably had little reason to be interested in the City pages of even the *Sun* or *Mirror.* 'It's Sir Stafford's company,' she said, 'Transport, Road and Overseas Development. I got a job there today.'

There was a pause.

'Have you been drinking, Miss?' Inspector Fulwell asked. He bent suspiciously over the carpet.

'This is where you say the body was?'

'There was another carpet on top. A rug. The body was on that. There must have been blood. I didn't move him to look.'

'Quite,' the inspector said.

He drew a black notebook from his pocket as though it was a weapon and opened it very carefully. He took out a ballpoint pen and very slowly and precisely wrote something.

'Ah,' Gaylord Poyntz said, watching him, 'the heavy hand of the law.'

'Shut up,' Fanny said. 'This is a neighbour,' she explained to the inspector.

'Oh, indeed?' he said. From his expression Fanny could see that he had taken an instant dislike to Gaylord.

Inspector Fulwell turned to the sergeant. 'Kerslake, use the car radio. Check this Barrow or Burroughs out, will you? And this TROD fellow. Sir Stafford Williams, did you say? See if we've anything on them, will you?'

Kerslake nodded and went out. They listened to the sound of his footsteps on the gravel as he set off up the lane to the High Street where they would have had to leave the car.

'Inconvenient place to bring a body, really, isn't it?' Gaylord Poyntz said in the tone of one who makes polite conversation to strangers.

Inspector Fulwell raised an eyebrow.

Gaylord said, 'I mean, if you were just putting it out of the way till you could clear it up.'

'It's quite easy to get in and out from the back, through the car park,' Fanny said. 'And quiet, too, once the pub closes.' Her voice petered out. She suddenly realized that she sounded defensive, and it was a queer thing to find herself defending her home as a convenient murder site.

'Did you see the body, sir?' Inspector Fulwell asked Gaylord. He left a small pause before the sir, which made it sound sarcastic.

'Poyntz,' he said. 'I can spell that for you, if necessary. US citizen, age 38. You want my social security number? And no, I didn't.'

Inspector Fulwell's expression dismissed Gaylord as a person of no possible interest, except that his presence here somehow confirmed Fanny's guilt. They waited in silence. There was the faint sound of Sergeant Kerslake's returning footsteps. The sergeant opened the front door, stepped carefully down into the lobby, and said 'Excuse me, madam' as he passed Fanny and went directly to the inspector. He handed him a note written on lined paper torn from a notebook.

Inspector Fulwell read it. He sighed. He looked at Fanny with distaste he made no effort to disguise.

'Well, Miss Dinmont, it seems you have the

second sight,' he said. 'It seems your Mr Burroughs is indeed deceased.'

'Of course he's dead. That's what I've been trying to tell you. He was lying there quite, quite dead on my sitting-room floor just an hour ago.'

'I don't know what game you think you're playing, Miss Dinmont, but I hardly think that's likely. The unfortunate Mr Burroughs was involved in a very nasty car crash on the Rowfield bypass less than half an hour ago. A head-on collision with a lorry. Mr Burroughs was in Sir Stafford Williams's Jaguar car.'

'What a country,' Gaylord said. 'It shouldn't be allowed, driving after death.'

'For your information, Mr Poyntz, Mr Burroughs was not driving Sir Stafford's car. Sir Stafford himself was driving. Mr Burroughs was the passenger, and very foolishly he was not wearing a seatbelt.'

Inspector Fulwell's expression stated that Mr Burroughs deserved his fate.

'He went through the windscreen,' he said with a hint of reverent satisfaction, 'death was instantaneous.'

'Well rehearsed, though,' Gaylord muttered.

'Sir Stafford? Was Sir Stafford hurt?' Fanny asked quickly in a loud voice.

Sergeant Kerslake answered her.

'Apparently not. Sir Stafford did a rather foolish thing, I'm afraid. According to our witness he ran away from the scene of the accident. We're looking for him now.'

'Who's your witness?' Gaylord asked. 'The driver of the lorry?'

'I believe so, sir,' Sergeant Kerslake said.

Fanny sat down on the arm of the settee. She couldn't take in what the inspector had said.

'Look, Inspector, I know what you must be thinking. I know you think I've wasted your time. But there was a body on my floor, I know there was. And it was Mr Burroughs. What's happening here?'

The inspector said, 'It's an extraordinary thing, Miss Dinmont. I'd wonder if you were being mischievous, if you already knew of the accident, but then there'd have been so little point. Unless, of course, you have a warped sense of humour.'

He paused for a moment. 'But your call was apparently received before the accident happened. Or so it seems,' he added in a tone of deep suspicion.

'For God's sake, you've got to believe me.'

Fanny could hear herself sounding hysterical.

Her hands were shaking. Something wet was dripping on her blouse. She looked and saw that she was spilling the glass of whisky she had in her trembling hand.

Inspector Fulwell too was looking at her. It was a look that said plainly that he thought she was either a liar or not all there.

CHAPTER THREE

Fanny insisted she would be perfectly capable of staying alone in a cottage where a dead body had been found.

Then Gaylord left, and she found that she wasn't by any means capable of it.

She ran after him, slipping in the mud where the cars going into the Deans' garage workshop had churned up the lane. Until then she had almost forgotten her cold wet feet, but now the chill mud soaked her shoes all over again. She cursed Gaylord for leaving her behind; she cursed the police; she nearly cursed poor Mr Burroughs for getting himself killed on her living-room carpet and causing the shenanigans of the night, but she stopped herself with the thought that he, poor man, was in a colder place than she was.

She caught up with Gaylord at the main road and grabbed his arm.

'You're a proper bastard, Mr Poyntz,' she said, 'you should've known I couldn't stay there alone,' and then she added, 'that's odd.'

'What is? Me being a proper bastard? Not really.'

'Over there. See?'

She pointed across the High Street to where an antiques business had taken over four of the beautiful golden brick houses and knocked doors through their interconnecting walls as a showroom. Behind the elegant period facades the rare and expensive furniture and porcelain was displayed as part of a perfect domestic setting, like a giant doll's house. Panelled walls and moulded ceilings advertised a peripheral business of the antiques dealer.

'Bentham's lights are on,' Fanny said.

Gaylord glanced up impatiently, pulling her across the street.

'They're always on. They leave them on all night to deter burglars. And presumably there's always the chance that a megalomaniac millionaire might pass by and decide the entire stock is exactly what he needs for his house in the Hamptons.'

'I know, but that's not the point. They were off when I went out to phone earlier.'

'A power cut.'

'Did the lights go off in the telephone box?'

'No. It's probably on a different circuit. I don't know. What difference does it make?'

'We could soon tell. The clock on my cooker will have stopped.'

'The clock on my cooker will have stopped too. But the one in my internal alcohol intake monitoring unit hasn't, so let's check there.'

The Manor House was set back from a lane off the High Street, a square, precise stone house lovingly measured by its eighteenth-century builder. There were two tall windows on the ground floor evenly spaced on either side of the pillared portico, and in the storey above a fifth casement giving out on to the small terrace made by the flat roof of the portico. The house stood behind a ten-foot wrought iron railing with an arched gate, with a sweep of gravel to the front door. Fanny had been curious about the house since she first came to the village; it seemed so self-contained among a cluster of later Victorian homes and modern bungalows. Once or twice when she walked by she had heard dogs barking; occasionally in the summer the sound of tennis balls hit hard, and the hum of a motor mower droning down the slope towards the river behind the house; she knew the man who lived there was called Hughes but she had never actually seen anyone there. The Manor House seemed to her out of tune with the jolly, jam-making, gossipy style of the rest of the village.

Gaylord Poyntz heaved the wrought iron gate open enough for her to squeeze through the gap. He took her elbow to lead her across the gravel to the front door, skirting a car she brushed against as they passed.

'Careful, don't touch that,' Gaylord said in alarm. 'That's an almost antique Buick you're messing with.'

'A great lump of a car like that shouldn't be in a small space like this,' Fanny said. 'Why don't you buy a field for it?'

'It's not mine. It comes with the house.'

Inside the front door it felt colder than in the night outside. Gaylord turned on a light. They were in a pale-painted hallway lined with pictures. The staircase rose to a landing draped with tapestries. The light was a branching electrolier on a brass chain, which cast shivering shadows as it swung slightly in the draught from the front door.

'Wow!' Fanny said.

'None of it has anything to do with me,' Gaylord said. 'I don't think any of it has much to do with Harry either. He's the guy who owns it. Harry's in New York making himself a couple more million.'

'What about the car?'

'The Buick? I told you, that's his too.'

He plunged through double doors on the left and disappeared. She heard the sound of a cork being drawn.

'It's red, OK?' he called. 'You have the wine. I'll stick to whisky. I've been on it for twenty years and I think at last it may be doing some good.'

She followed the sound of his voice. The room she entered was sparsely furnished. A small table, two sofas with legs like gazelles', and several spindly upright chairs were scattered on the polished wood floor as though they had never been introduced. To her left, looking blankly into the darkness, the two tall casement windows were framed by elaborately draped curtains held back by tasselled bands.

At the opposite end of the room, a full-length gilded mirror reflected the dark outline of Gaylord Poyntz holding glasses full of liquid the same rich colours as the robes of the shadowy figure of a woman in an oil painting above the pink-tinged marble fireplace. Fanny was suddenly struck by how good-looking he was. She'd always been attracted by the smouldering, dark, poetical look in men, but in the mirror Gaylord's hawkish profile seemed particularly mysterious and romantic.

'Here,' he said, 'get this down you.'

He pushed the bottle towards her across the polished mahogany surface. He watched her drink, following her eyes as she looked at the painting. 'Harry likes pretending that's his last duchess up there. What a bitch, eh?'

'This room is beautiful.'

'Yeah, but somehow I feel like a roach in an operating theatre.'

Fanny wished she hadn't come. She felt out of place. But she was afraid to go home. It made her start shaking again to think of the clean space on her mushroom carpet where the body of Mr Burroughs had been. She wanted to put off facing that until daylight. At least Gaylord Poyntz was warm and rude and tweedy, even if it was clear he would prefer she wasn't there.

He got up and brought the dwindling bottle of red wine to fill her glass, sitting down beside her on the sofa.

'It's all right, you know. You don't have to go if you don't want to. We can sit here and get drunk.'

'I just don't want to go home,' she said.

'Look,' he said, 'we've got to think. You *did* see a body, you aren't mad are you? I mean certifiably insane, not just jibbering like the rest of us normals? Let's agree you're not mad. You saw a body. It disappeared. Your carpet disappeared. There was a murder. Also theft of a carpet, hardly used, only one corpse. But as far as the police are concerned, the murder victim was killed in a simple but unpleasant traffic accident.'

'I thought you didn't believe me.'

'Well, I didn't really think about it one way or the other at first. But then I saw you weren't lying. I've seen a lot of women lying, usually to me, and when they do they all have the same look on their faces. They have a look of complete sincerity. I know you're not lying, you've never looked sincere enough to be lying. And if there's a corpse goes missing in your carpet and turns up in a car crash some time later, sans carpet, then someone's got to do something about it. Know what I mean?'

'Thanks,' Fanny said. 'I was beginning to wonder myself.'

She suddenly felt tremendously relieved, and very tired.

'We'll talk about it in the morning,' Gaylord said. 'Meanwhile, another drink.'

He began to talk about cartooning. He made jokes, speaking in funny voices. He was amusing and very good-looking but she was exhausted.

Fanny didn't know when she fell asleep. She woke up in the morning with the sun playing on her face, streaming through the french window so brightly that through the dusty smeared glass she could see nothing. She was lying on the sofa, covered with a blanket coated with grey dog hairs. She was stiff, with a slight stabbing pain behind her left eye reminding her of the red wine she had drunk. Her shoes stood on the floor beside the sofa, the still-wet leather already contorted and dull. The sun cast shimmering bands of bright dust into the room. She screwed up her eyes as they watered.

Fanny threw open the french window and stepped out on to a terrace at the back of the house. The air was cool and damp. Dew spangled the network of spiders' webs which lay like gauze on the grass of the lawn. There was a tennis court beyond.

From inside the house she heard barking. Her watch had stopped. The church clock chimed seven. She shivered and went back into the elegant drawing-room. She folded the blanket. There was no sign of the wine bottles or the empty glasses of the night before. Without them there seemed to be no clues about the nature of the man who was living here. And Gaylord's mysterious friend Harry hadn't left any finger-prints either, no photographs, no books, the furniture bought in a job lot. The mysterious Harry was passing through just like Gaylord. Suddenly Fanny felt rootless and frightened. Annoyingly, she missed her ex-husband Alan. Alan had given her roots, and roots were something she felt she needed right now.

She left the folded blanket on a sturdy carved chest in the hall. She let herself out of the house, closing the door carefully behind her.

The village street was still sunk in sleep. Mist clung to the roofs of the houses. There was no one about; it was too early even for the paper boy. She walked as quietly as she could down the lane past the cottages of which her own was the last in a thatched terrace. From the bedroom windows on a level with the top of her head she could hear the muffled sounds of her neighbours waking, a radio playing, bedsprings easing as someone got up. It was just another Saturday morning. There was a sense of a luxurious lack of hurry.

In her cottage the sun streamed through the sliding glass door where Gaylord had left the curtain open when he checked her footsteps on the lawn. She heard the click of the thermostat as the central heating boiler turned itself off. At least the place was warm now. The fridge hummed. Somewhere a sleepy bluebottle took off, buzzed briefly and disappeared. Fanny felt as though Mr Burroughs' body, the police, and Gaylord himself, were unreal, hangovers from a dream.

She sat in the big wicker peacock chair, one of the first things she and Alan had bought for the cottage, and stared into the garden as she sipped coffee. Next door the baby started to cry. A line of slightly steaming nappies hung dripping from a clothes line above the fence which divided her neighbours' garden from hers. She shuddered. Poor young Mrs Dean, she thought, a slave to twins and another child under four. Fanny had not yet hankered for the joys of motherhood and she saw no reason why she ever should now. As far as she could see, young Mrs Dean didn't get much pleasure out of it, but being part of the largest and oldest tribe in the village, she'd probably never had much choice.

Fanny tried to think of other things, even of Alan, but do what she would, her eyes kept returning to the blank, oddly-clean, rectangle on the mushroom carpet at her feet. Maybe there hadn't been a body. She might be going mad. She wondered if she herself believed any longer what she had seen last night. It had been a traumatic day, there'd been the job interview, then the excitement of being offered a salary which meant she could keep up the mortgage payments on the London flat without needing to sell this cottage which she'd taken as her share in the divorce settlement. People who lost their jobs, she'd read, lost their identity, and felt they couldn't prove that they existed any more. Without a job, without Alan, afraid of losing the cottage or her London flat, Fanny thought that she had already begun to doubt her own reality. It wasn't surprising that getting work again could cause some sort of psychological upheaval, hallucinations, or memory blanks.

She tried to remember more about her meeting with poor Mr Burroughs. What had he actually said as they chatted while she waited for Sir Stafford to finish his call? She'd mentioned the cottage. No, he had. He'd glanced at the paper with the details of her career she'd sent to TROD after she'd had the letter asking if she'd be interested in the job. Mr Burroughs had known Rowfield. A lovely area, he'd said. He'd looked wistful, because she remembered wondering where he lived, imagining him in some prim suburban terrace in a faceless town near a Southern Region station. He'd said he used to walk by the river round Rowfield, he'd drunk beer at The Black Bull. He'd been an undergraduate at Oxford. He'd made a joke about how long ago it was, and how things must have changed.

Fanny recalled him sitting beside her, impeccable in his old-fashioned three-button suit and shiny black shoes. He'd offered her a cigarette and automatically flicked a speck of loose tobacco into his palm and dusted it into an ashtray. It would drive you mad to live with him, she'd thought.

But even if he was a meticulous man with old-fashioned manners, he would not, on coming round after falling and hitting his head in her house, have rolled up the carpet to take away and have it cleaned. Not without leaving a note he wouldn't.

Young Mrs Dean next door came out into her garden, tested the nappies with one hand, and turned to feed her rabbits. Fanny caught her eye through the sliding door. Young Mrs Dean smiled and waved. Fanny opened the door and called, 'Hallo, how are you? How're the babies? Your washing won't take long to dry today, I should think.'

Young Mrs Dean closed the rabbit hutch. 'Long way to go yet. They got drenched overnight.'

'You're early today,' Fanny said, pulling at a rampant dockweed thrusting between the flagstones on her patio.

'Oh, there's a big stir today. Michael told us, and we had to go out and take a look. Bentham's been robbed.' Young Mrs Dean flushed with excitement.

'Bentham's! Did they lose a lot?'

Young Mrs Dean was enjoying herself. Fanny could tell she was thinking that Bentham's could afford to lose some of its treasures. Things like that were better turned into money which could benefit some poor body.

'Well,' she said, 'our John went down there when the police came and they said they thought it must be boys from the estate. They just smashed the window and messed about a bit inside, but it seems they didn't get away with much.'

She sounded disappointed. Fanny understood this was not out of malice for Bentham's, but because greater loss or damage would have made a better story.

'I must say myself I'm surprised if it was lads from the estate,' she went on. 'John said they'd cut off the electric to stop the alarm, and then turned it on again when they left, so they don't sound like young vandals to me.'

'Did you hear anything last night? Here, I mean. Anyone moving about?'

'Ah, bless you, no, there's no call for you to worry. They wouldn't come down this way, would they? You never hear anything down here at night. John and me had the telly on and we never heard nothing. Come to think on it, he did say he heard you come in, but that's all.' Mrs Dean was embarrassed, because in fact her John had made a coarse comment about it sounding like Fanny had brought a fellow down with her at last, and she didn't think it would be proper to mention it. She changed tack. 'I don't know as how you're not scared coming in alone at night like you do. I wouldn't dare go in there alone, that I wouldn't.'

Fanny laughed to show bravado. 'Oh, I'm not afraid down here. In London it's different. There are parts of London I'd never walk alone at night.'

London was too remote a concept for young Mrs Dean. 'Fancy that now,' she said, and they both sighed at the state of the world. 'Well, this won't get my work done,' she said.

As Fanny went back into the house there was a loud knock at the front door. Gaylord Poyntz stood there. He was trying to unravel the leads of two excited small grey dogs fighting at his feet.

'I thought I'd give them a chance to stretch their legs before the pubs open,' he said. 'I thought because they have such short legs they wouldn't need to walk very far, but they're midget marathon runners. Anyway, I was passing and it seemed like a good idea to see how you're getting on after last night.'

Fanny stood back to let him in. The dogs jumped at her. She bent down to stroke them.

'The grey one's Bertie and the greyer one's Jeeves,' Gaylord said. He held on to their leads to try and stop them jumping up at her.

'Oh, let them go,' Fanny said. 'Maybe they'll dig up a new corpse for me. My old one's run off.'

'Any conclusions?' he asked.

'I don't know. It's hard to believe, looking

round here in the light of day.'

'Sure it is. But could you really make up a thing like that? You don't seem to be a woman of unfettered imaginings or raving tendencies.'

'But even your dogs don't bother sniffing the carpet where the body was, do they?'

The two terriers were in the garden now.

Ah, the analytical mind at work,' Gaylord said. 'Never mind the psychologist. The dogs made straight for the garden. Do you know anything about dog psychology?'

'Sure I do. They sniff at carpets where dead bodies have been.'

'There was another carpet on top, remember. Calculated to deceive the keenest nose of dog. Still, you're right, you'd expect the passing once-over.'

'Perhaps they're just dim,' Fanny said.

They both looked out into the garden for the dogs.

'Bertie!' Gaylord shouted, going to the glass door. 'He's got something in his mouth. What is it?'

Fanny made a quick prayer that it would not be one of young Mrs Dean's rabbits.

Bertie, wagging his tail, brought his prize to Gaylord's feet and dropped it. Gaylord bent to look at it before he picked it up.

'Will you look at this!' he said.

It was a brass candlestick. Fanny took it, then almost dropped it. Its square base was caked with dry, dark blood.

Bertie scrabbled at her legs, barking, expecting her to throw the thing for him.

'Is it yours?' Gaylord asked.

'No, it isn't mine.' She was whispering.

'Well,' Gaylord said slowly, 'whoever lost this will be out looking for it. It's quite valuable, you know.'

'For God's sake, don't you know what it is?'

'Sure I do. An eighteenth century brass candlestick, one of a pair. In good condition, too.'

'It's blood. Blood, for God's sake!'

'Which makes it very valuable indeed to someone.'

High in the sky, a small plane went suddenly into a dive, twirling soundlessly before the engine coughed and it began to climb. The two dogs were standing expectantly at Gaylord's feet. He glanced up at the Deans' bedroom window, then took Fanny's elbow and pushed her back into the house. He slid the door shut on the two eager dark Cairn faces.

'I wonder where the dog found it?' Fanny's voice was unsteady.

'You could do with a drink,' he said.

'The police!' Fanny said. 'We've got to tell the police. They can check the blood with Mr Burroughs' DNA to prove he was here.'

Gaylord spread a blue-spotted handkerchief on the coffee table and laid the candlestick on it. They both stared at it, with its ugly stain on the base.

In the garden the dogs wrestled. Along the lane, outside the kitchen window, they heard a snatch of conversation as a group of women walked down to buy eggs and vegetables from the Faulkners further down the path. Fanny waited for them to pass, then went out of the cottage to telephone the police. But in the High Street there were two squad cars parked outside Bentham's. A policeman stood stolidly between two graceful stone figures of Venus on decorative plinths at the shop entrance.

Fanny recognized Constable Mimms. She crossed the road to speak to him.

Yes, Inspector Fulwell was there, but he was busy at the moment. When he was free, yes, he would be very interested to know that Miss Dinmont had found a murder weapon. What murder would that be, Miss? Yes, he would tell the inspector.

'Don't you understand?' Fanny sounded fierce. 'The murder weapon complete with blood and whatever else shows up under forensic examination when people investigate a fatal blow. It's in my sitting-room, and whoever left it in my garden knows it's incriminating evidence and will want it back when he knows it's been found. You understand what I'm saying, don't you? He's already killed once, and certainly won't let another little murder stand in his way.'

'If you say so, Miss,' Constable Mimms said.

He watched her turn angrily away. He made

no effort to hide his thoughts. Fanny knew that he was thinking, I fancy that, it's a pity she's cracked. 'Jerk,' she said, but under her breath.

Exasperated, Fanny went home. This time she walked through The Black Bull car park in order to avoid her neighbours in the lane. She banged her garden gate, and then remembered the dogs. She expected them to rush at her.

But they were not there. She ran across the lawn and pulled back the glass door, thinking Gaylord must have taken them into the house. The room was empty.

And the gruesome thing that had been lying on a blue-spotted handkerchief on the coffee table was gone.

CHAPTER FOUR

There was a shout from the garden. 'Fanny!'

Gaylord, the two dogs at his heel, came into the garden leaving the gate open behind him.

'Fanny, I'm here!'

After a feeling of relief Fanny was furious.

'Where've you been?' she said.

'I went for a drink.'

'You did what?'

'A drink. I needed a drink.'

He was carrying a bottle.

Fanny was speechless. He'd left the cottage unguarded without a thought and someone had come in and taken the murder weapon away.

Gaylord went into the kitchen and came back with a tumbler. He opened the bottle of whisky and half-filled the glass.

'Drink this,' he said.

'Gaylord . . .' She gestured towards the coffee table. He drank straight from the whisky bottle.

There was something wrong with a man who drank this much. He wasn't the sort of ally she needed in a desperate situation.

'Drink it,' he said.

'I don't want it.'

'You will. It's gone. The evidence.'

'You mean they came while you were here?'

'Not exactly.'

There was a loud knocking at the front door.

'My God, that's the police,' Fanny said. 'They've come to see the murder weapon. What am I going to say to them?'

'Leave it to me.'

He pushed past her and opened the front door. His bulk filled the lobby and she could not see past him. She went back into the sitting-room and took a quick drink of the whisky to steady herself while Gaylord stood talking in a low voice to the policemen.

Gaylord led Inspector Fulwell and Sergeant Kerslake into the dining area.

'Well, Miss Dinmont?' Inspector Fulwell

said. He sounded hostile.

Fanny resented his tone. After all, she thought, I'm only trying to help his inquiries.

'It's Mrs, not Miss,' she said. 'I'm Mrs Dinmont.'

'I apologize,' Inspector Fulwell said. 'Is Mr Dinmont lost, stolen, or strayed?'

Fanny supposed that this was meant to be a joke.

'What about this murder weapon, Mrs Dinmont?'

'But didn't Mr Poyntz tell you? How the dog found it, and now it's gone again. Didn't he explain?'

'Steady on, Fanny,' Gaylord said, 'of course I explained.'

'In the circumstances you're fortunate I'm not putting you on a charge. You can thank Mr Poyntz for that. People like you need treatment.'

He looked at her with disgust. Fanny backed away, tripping over the edge of the coffee table. She spilled the whisky.

She was shocked by his manner, then angry. 'Now look here, Inspector,' she said, 'there's no need for you to take that tone with me. It's not my fault the thing disappeared. Or that some murderer dumped a dead body in my house.'

'I have no wish to discuss it,' Inspector Fulwell said. 'I'm sure I'm as liberal as the next man, but people like that are a menace in society.'

Fanny looked at Gaylord in amazement.

'They should be put somewhere for their own good where they can't do any harm,' Inspector Fulwell said. He breathed out sharply as though he would rather have spat. Sergeant Kerslake was nodding his head.

'Goodbye, Mrs Dinmont,' the inspector said. 'Come along, Sergeant, we've got work to do.' He turned and walked out of the front door. The sergeant nodded at Fanny, then at Gaylord, and followed.

Fanny turned on Gaylord.

'What the hell was all that about? What did you tell him? And what's going on? Where's the candlestick?'

Gaylord looked doubtful. He reached for the bottle.

'You may not like this much,' he said, 'but it was the best I could do at short notice. I told him you're a drunk. That you're very confused and see things, imagine things that aren't there.'

'*You* told them *I'm* a drunk? And they *believed you?*'

Gaylord sat down on the settee and took a swig from the bottle. 'They're policemen, Fanny. They follow clues. You were drinking when they came in. Your breath smelled of it. And the drunken way you're behaving, reporting stolen dead bodies and non-existent murder weapons.'

'But it's not non-existent. You know it isn't?'

'Quite. But I didn't tell them that.'

'You didn't tell them?'

Something horrible was going on here. She edged away, but Gaylord began to laugh.

'No, but I got rid of the candlestick.'

'You did what? Why?'

Gaylord began to pace the room. He was long-legged and he looked absurd with his three steps to the coffee table and three back to the staircase. Fanny noticed for the first time that he had to walk slightly hunched to keep his head from hitting the ceiling.

'It just suddenly seemed the best way of letting the whole thing blow over,' he said. 'You know, and I believe you, that someone killed Mr Burroughs. That someone is not a nice man. It struck me that if there's no sign the police think there's been a murder, the murderer will leave the weapon where it was. Why bother finding it, if there's nothing to hide? But if you start a murder hunt by finding a murder weapon . . .' he paused, 'well, I thought you'd be safer.'

'Are you crazy? You are crazy! What did you do with it?'

'Exactly what I imagine the murderer did when he heard you coming. Flung it into the undergrowth. It's obvious you don't do much gardening.'

'You realize that was our best hope of proving there was a murder?'

'Fanny, the police are convinced Mr Burroughs died in the car. You are the only one who knows he didn't. Can't you imagine the danger that puts you in?'

'But the candlestick might have had the murderer's prints on it.'

'I don't think he'd be that careless.'

'I think you're crazy. I'm getting the hell out of here.'

Fanny wrenched open the sliding door. The dogs began to jump at her.

'I'll come with you,' Gaylord said, 'We can take the dogs down to the river. Then you can drive us out to The Boathook pub. I'll buy you lunch and I'll try to explain everything.'

After all, she thought, it was better to have someone with her in a situation like this, even Gaylord Poyntz. But she didn't trust him. Why should she? He had popped up out of nowhere. She didn't know anything about him and his friend Harry was another complete stranger to the village. There was no one to vouch for either of them. All she knew was what he'd told her, and there was no reason why she should think he was telling the truth.

Suddenly she found herself wishing that Alan was there with her instead. He had been unfaithful, he had lied to her, but she always knew when he was lying and that at least was something she could rely on.

'It had better be good,' Fanny said.

CHAPTER FIVE

The Boathook was an old pub beside the river out in the country. In the evening the bar would be crowded with groups of trendy young people from nearby towns, but now there were only a few middle-aged couples and a group of oddly similar young women sitting round a table over a bottle of wine. Their flowing clothes smelled strongly of incense which hung round their table. Fanny heard Gaylord muttering as they made their way between the tables towards the bar.

'Weaned on pickles,' he said, 'what a coven of witches.'

'Shut up,' Fanny said.

She recognized one of the women. Melanie something or other, she'd remember later. Melanie had been a useful contact when a magazine had commissioned Fanny to write a series of articles about topical countryside issues.

Fanny saw that Melanie had heard that Gaylord crack about witches for she glanced up and gave him a look of contempt through her small round steel-rimmed spectacles. But the look changed to interest. Lustful interest, Fanny thought. Then Melanie saw Fanny and pushed her long, thin, pale hair away from her cosmetic-free face and smiled. Fanny waved at her.

'My God,' Gaylord said, 'do you actually know that woman?'

'She's an environmental campaigner,' Fanny said. 'They protest about issues like pollution and new roads and animal rights. My new job is going to involve a lot of dialogue with people like Melanie.'

Gaylord bought a bottle of wine and she led the way to a table in a far corner. He banged his head on a beam.

'It's like being in a coffin,' he said.

'I wonder when Mr Burroughs' funeral will be?' Fanny said, 'and if Sir Stafford will be there. Or if he'll still be fleeing the scene of the accident. I suppose I'll be in the middle of it, trying to explain if he doesn't turn up. It's not the sort of public relations I imagined. Well, Monday morning will be the real test for Sir Stafford. A man like that, if he's not at his desk first thing in the morning, there's something much more serious stopping him than running away after a car crash.'

She didn't say much during lunch. She kept thinking about her new job and how hard it was going to be with this totally unexpected turn up, but mostly she thought about Mr Burroughs and the bloody candlestick.

'Hey!' Gaylord said, 'have the sinister sisters put a spell on you?'

'Sorry, I was thinking. Let's get out of here.'

She couldn't eat now, not with pictures of

Mr Burroughs in her head.

They let the excited dogs out of the car and followed the sound of their yapping along the river path. A slight wind stirred the leaves of the willow trees and rustled the dried husk of rushes under the bank. The river was low at the end of summer, and where it flowed fast, green weed fanned out like a woman's hair on the water.

Fanny leaned against a fallen willow trunk and stared into an amber pool. She was suddenly aware of Gaylord close beside her. Embarrassed, she leaned away.

'What is this job of yours?' he asked. 'What did you do before it?'

'Oh, I was a freelance journalist. I don't suppose I made enough to support myself without Alan—that's the ex-Mr Dinmont—but it was fun. I gave up a staff job when I married him.'

'The ex-Mr Dinmont, is he dead?'

'No, he just smells bad.'

'What happened?'

Fanny threw a willow twig into the current and watched as it was whirled away.

'Nothing. Nothing happened at all. He was in advertising. Then he met an American girl.'

'So he left?'

'Sure he left. Don't take it personally, but I've got a grudge against American women.'

'You! You've got a grudge against American women! What about me? You weren't married to Miss Gila Monster Gulch 1997.'

They were all the same, trying to make jokes of the women they'd married, once they weren't married to them anymore. Fanny thought Alan probably made a joke out of her.

Gaylord was asking about TROD. She told him that Sir Stafford had hired her because he was worried the company appeared to the outside world almost like a secret society in a political climate that demanded openness. He wanted to give it a more friendly face.

Fanny funked telling Gaylord that Alan had got her the job, and then she did. Gaylord didn't say anything, but she knew he must be thinking that Alan getting her the job was pretty pathetic.

The thought of work seemed to dispel the peace of the river. The sun was suddenly not as warm and the wind flattened the rushes. Fanny shivered.

Gaylord whistled to the dogs.

'Come on,' he said, 'let's go back. These little bastards must have had enough exercise for one day.'

She stopped the car outside the mysterious Harry's gates. She had never seen them open.

'Come on in,' he said. 'You can make a token cup of tea if you must, but a good Scotch will warm you up.'

The hall was dim even at mid-afternoon. Gaylord led the way past the staircase and down a brief passage into a large kitchen with a flagged floor and wooden draining boards. In the chimney recess stood a yellowing Aga cooker. From a window above the vast enamelled sink the garden unfolded to the river, an overgrown tangle of nettles and defiant hollyhocks. A pollarded willow marked the edge of the stream.

'I wonder what Harry thought he was buying into when he took this place,' Gaylord said. 'To look at him, you'd think he's just an ordinary multi-millionaire obsessed by greed, but I guess he must have a romantic streak. He should have a butler here, a Beach who suffers from his feet.'

'A Wodehouse buff! You *are* an Anglophile Yank.'

'Wodehouse,' Gaylord said stiffly, 'became an American citizen. I collect him. First editions.'

'I collect things too.'

'You do? What things?'

Icon things.'

'Gee, and there's me—an iconoclast.'

The kitchen was warm. They sat in two old armchairs by the Aga. The dogs lay quietly in their baskets beside it. Fanny studied Gaylord. Is he frightened, she thought, or doesn't he want to be bothered? Is that why he threw the murder weapon away? Perhaps he really did it to protect me. She found herself smiling at the thought.

But there was another explanation. He

could be the murderer! It was a frightening thought, but she was too tired to be frightened.

'Let's go through what we know already,' Gaylord was saying.

It occurred to her that he seemed to be reading her mind. She deliberately kept her tone frivolous. 'About P.G. Wodehouse?' she said. 'Or about icons?'

He shook his head. 'This is serious.'

'I suppose destroying criminal evidence isn't serious?'

'I didn't destroy it. I put it away for safe keeping. Sherlock Holmes was always doing that sort of thing.'

'So we agree we can't drop it? The murder of Mr Burroughs?'

'I didn't exactly say that, but what do we have? Let's see, Mr B., quiet, inoffensive man of about sixty-five, no known vices, worked closely with Sir Stafford Williams, who has disappeared, but when not disappeared, runs a rather convoluted conglomerate with vast overseas interests.'

Fanny nodded.

'Sir Stafford sounds like the key to this,' Gaylord said. 'Does he have strong political affiliations that you know of, anything sinister like that?'

Fanny looked blank. She had no idea. Sir Stafford was not the kind of multi-millionaire who courted public notice. She knew nothing about him personally.

'You see,' Gaylord said, 'Sir Stafford could be the intended victim, don't you think? They got Burroughs by mistake. Lots of people must want to kill Sir Stafford.'

And since he's disappeared,' Fanny said, 'perhaps they've corrected the mistake.'

'My thoughts exactly, Watson.'

'Which means the end of my promising career and my dream cottage,' Fanny said.

That's the awful thing when something happens to a man like Sir Stafford, she thought, it affects so many people's lives. You can simply feel sorry for old Mr Burroughs. Then she said aloud and out of context, 'Sir Stafford's years older than Mr B, but it's never "Old Sir Stafford".'

'Are you sure you haven't been drinking?' Gaylord asked, giving her a funny look. 'Or am I wrong, and you really are a raving lunatic?'

'Sorry, I was just thinking.'

'Well, so far there's not much to go on. What do we know? This old guy Burroughs meets you and decides to come down and visit you in the middle of the night. Don't think me ungallant, but why? Can we dismiss your irresistible sex appeal?'

'I think we can. But he did know I was coming down here because he said something about celebrating, and I said I might go into Oxford and buy a nineteenth-century St George icon I'd seen in a little shop there some time ago. And he said yes, he saw I collected icons in my CV, but weren't they terribly rare and valuable, and I said they could be, but mine weren't. And he said that was nice and how anyway I could enjoy my weekend in Rowfield without being afraid of the wicked bank foreclosing now I'd got the job. Perhaps he wanted to tell me something.'

'Tell you something?'

'Well, Sir Stafford was with him, according to the police. Maybe we got this wrong and Sir Stafford is the bad guy. Maybe he got wind of what Burroughs wanted to tell me and it was dynamite and he had to stop him at any price, so he followed him down to the cottage and killed him in a panic.'

'Then how did Mr Burroughs get here? He was in Sir Stafford's car.'

'Maybe they'll find Burroughs' car in Rowfield. But probably not. The evil-doers will have taken it away.' Then Fanny added, 'It seems rather strange, a frail old financial wizard like Sir Stafford suddenly killing a man and carting his corpse around in my carpet.'

The late afternoon sun was fading. Shadows eclipsed the edges of the kitchen. Fanny and Gaylord drew closer to the stove. Gaylord stretched out his long legs and his knees creaked.

'I'm getting old,' he said, 'if I'm going to murder anyone and play hide and seek with the corpse I'd best put my mind to it and do it now, although all I want to murder now is a drink.'

'What about the robbery?' Fanny said. She had forgotten about the break-in at Bentham's. 'Do you think there's a connection?'

'Could be. Piers—you know Piers, who runs the place?—I saw him in the pub this morning when I was buying medicinal hooch to ply you with. He said that whatever the police say, he thinks it looked more like a search than a robbery.'

'It says something for modern education if vandals are breaking into antiques shops just to look at the beautiful things.'

'There's no proof it was vandals. One thug breaks a window very much like another. You realize you're accepting a class assumption?' He paused. 'Hey,' he said, 'did you ever think of this? Sir Stafford and Burroughs are a team, crazed collectors. They're bored buying things, so they start stealing the stuff, to add spice. But on this particular caper they have a falling out. Sir Stafford is always hogging the best pieces. Burroughs wants the Georgian candlestick for himself. "Well, here, take it," Sir Stafford says and bags him over the head with it. Then he sees this joke has gone a bit far. He remembers his new minion, the beautiful Fanny Dinmont with the long legs, has a cottage in the village.'

'You noticed my legs, Sherlock? So you're not quite as old as you think you are.'

'I've a trained eye, my dear doctor. "So," Sir Stafford says, "I will deposit the corpse of my old playmate in her thatched . . ." '

'. . . Half-thatched . . .'

' ". . . half-thatched haven of peace and tranquillity." '

'Won't she notice?'

'Hell, you know what messy housekeepers these career girls are. But then he thinks again. The lovely Miss Dinmont might notice. He goes back and wraps old Burroughs in the rug, slings him over his shoulder, staggers up the fifty yards of the lane with corpse and carpet—say, how big is this guy Sir Stafford?'

'He'd make Woody Allen look like the Incredible Hulk.'

'Hm. Yes, hmm. Tosses the body into the trunk—the boot—of his car, and then drives said car into the path of a passing juggernaut, leaping out to safety at the last moment. Is there any chance this Sir Stafford is a spare-time commando or something? Yes, well, from where I'm sitting, I definitely think we can rule out suicide. What do you say, Miss Marple?'

Fanny stretched and yawned. 'I'm exhausted,' she said. I feel like I've been up dancing all night, seen the dawn and drunk too much.'

'Yeah, know the feeling. Let's go to bed.'

He stood up and pulled her to her feet.

'But, Mr Poyntz, what about your creaking knees?'

‘With your help, I can get upstairs,’ he said.

CHAPTER SIX

When Fanny sat up in bed and said she was hungry it was dark outside the uncurtained window.

‘That reminds me,’ Gaylord said, ‘I’m dying for a drink. I’ll throw in the whisky, but if you want to eat you’ll have to cook me dinner at your place, there isn’t a thing to eat here.’

The evening air was cool as they walked down the High Street and through the arch into The Black Bull car park. Lamps already shone behind closed blinds, and the blue-ish light of television glimmered through cracks in drawn curtains.

Fanny’s cottage was warm. There was a faint dry smell of undisturbed dust. She left him in the sitting-room and went into the kitchen to cook. She opened the window in the kitchen and the cool breeze wafted the scent of wood smoke into the sitting-room. The Faulkners must have had a bonfire, she thought. It made her feel strange, unsettled and insecure, that the happenings of an ordinary weekend were going on as normal.

Cooking was never a pleasure to her. Mostly she opened tins, and that’s what she did now, trying to disguise it with seasoning.

She heard a noise upstairs, or thought she did. It's nerves, she told herself, anyone would be a nervous wreck after opening the garden door and discovering a body on the floor. Who wouldn't be hearing things after that? And anyway, Gaylord was here, she wasn't alone.

'Jesus, you're no cook,' Gaylord said with something like respect when he saw what she had prepared. 'Maybe your Mr Dinmont's Miss America was a cook.'

Fanny laughed. To hell with calm and security, she was happy.

Then they sat together on the settee drinking whisky and black coffee.

'I like your icons,' he said.

So that was the noise she'd heard. He'd gone upstairs, poking round. She wanted to be cross but thought she wouldn't.

'Did you pick them up abroad?'

'Yes. I used to do a bit of travel writing, when I was on the permanent staff. Shall I show you?'

Fanny was conscious that she was trying too hard to entertain him. It's what happens, she thought, when you're intimate with someone you've only just met.

He followed her upstairs to the small front spare room. The icons were propped against the wall along an empty shelf.

Fanny noticed at once. She clutched Gaylord's arm.

'What is it? What's happened?' he asked.

'That icon! It isn't mine.'

She pointed at the strange icon. It stood between the St Michael she'd haggled over in an Istanbul market and the wing of a small triptych that Alan had given her when they first met.

She picked it up, turning it slowly over. It showed six saints arranged in two rows. Fanny thought one was St Paul, another St Stephen. She was puzzled by the curious wide-open black eyes and rolling eyeballs of all the saints. The back was dark, pitted wood cracked with age.

She handed it to Gaylord. He turned it this way and that, the light catching the gold of the saints' haloes. The icon was unlike any of hers, like a different art form. Fanny did not recognize the dusky figure of the dominant saint in the centre of the top row, nor any of the figures in the second rung.

'What do you make of it?' Gaylord asked.

She shook her head. 'I'm no expert. It's not like anything I've ever seen, not Greek or Russian.'

There was a pile of reference books on the floor. She began to search through them, then pulled out a heavy volume entitled *Icons.* She opened it and began to run through the pages of illustrations.

'Look,' she said, lifting the book to show Gaylord.

The icon illustrated had the same

formalized, static features, huge black eyes, dark crescent of hair under the golden halo, the same dense, exotic colourings.

'That's Coptic, from Ethiopia. What do you think?'

'It looks to me more like a cartoon than an icon,' Gaylord said, peering over her shoulder, 'except it's rare and wonderful. I didn't know the Ethiopians had icons.'

'Oh, yes, but you don't often see them. They're Coptic Christians. They're supposed to be one of the twelve tribes of Israel.'

She put down the book and took the icon from him.

'Look at the way the head's shaped, and the crudeness of the colours compared with this Greek one of mine. And these big stylized hands, all out of proportion.'

'It's amazing,' Gaylord said. 'Somebody must want you to have it.'

'Some *body*, you mean, don't you? It must've been poor Mr Burroughs. But it doesn't make sense.'

'A token of his regard, you think? Instead of a bunch of flowers. You told him you collected the things.'

'But a man like Mr Burroughs wouldn't own a thing like this. And if he'd been interested in them himself, he'd have said so.'

'Exactly. So why should he come down here in the middle of the night to leave a rare and wonderful Ethiopian icon in your cottage? Do you think he fell in love with your beautiful brown eyes?'

'They're not brown, they're hazel. Be serious! He must have wanted to hide it.' She stared at the icon. 'But why? Do you think he could've stolen it from Bentham's?' She shook her head. 'What am I going to do?'

'Perhaps you should call the police,' Gaylord said. 'I wouldn't mind seeing the look on Inspector Fulwell's face when you tell him you've got this collection of funny old wood paintings and suddenly there's an extra one which the man who was murdered in the cottage but died in a car crash miles away put in your spare room.'

'Don't joke,' she said. 'There's something weird going on.'

'Well, who knows you like icons and keep them here?'

'A few girlfriends who've stayed, I suppose, but I don't think any of them showed any interest. And Alan of course.'

'Ah, the former Mr Dinmont raises his ugly head!'

'I doubt if he even remembers I've got them. He knew they weren't valuable, so he took no notice. I think he thought my interest was one of those freakish feminine symptoms, like PMT. But he wasn't really ugly, he was quite good-looking before he began to put on weight.'

'So Miss America *was* a cook!'

Fanny put the strange icon back on the shelf.

'Come on,' she said, 'if there's someone watching this place, they'll wonder what we're doing in here all this time.'

'Yes, it would be perplexing for them, Watson, trying to figure what a man could be doing upstairs in a bedroom with a dark-haired beauty with incredibly long legs.'

'You must've thought me awfully easy.'

'Easy? Didn't you see me gasping for breath and shaking all over from exertion? But it's time I went. The dogs need a run. I shouldn't worry about being watched. They've most likely already been through this place. They'll have done that when they killed Burroughs, except you may have disturbed them.'

'You think they weren't sure what they were looking for?'

'Right, and one old bit of painted wood looked very like another to them.'

They went downstairs.

'Listen,' Gaylord said, 'after I've walked the dogs, should I—?'

'Yes,' Fanny said.

Later, she lay awake in the big brass bed, Gaylord asleep beside her. There was a full moon, the curtains were open and she looked out on the dark shapes of the hazel trees between her garden and the Faulkners. The wind tapped a loose strand of wisteria against the window pane like a nervous tic, while somewhere below young Mrs Dean's rabbits stamped their feet in their hutch.

She fell asleep and did not wake until the Sunday morning church bells started their peal for morning service at a quarter to ten.

Gaylord was not in the bed. She could hear him downstairs and she could smell coffee, real, not instant. He must have gone home and returned with it. And he'd brought the dogs with him. There was a tremendous scampering on the stairs and the two terriers leaped on the bed. Gaylord came up after them.

'Here's the story,' he said. 'Breakfast. Then in the bed. Lunch at the hotel. Then back to the bed to be beautified.'

'Ah,' she said, 'Cole Porter.'

'I promise not to sing unless you interrupt,' he said. 'Then walk these two, discuss corpses we have known, then dinner.'

Fanny did not mention that she had planned to leave that evening. I'll drive up early before the traffic tomorrow morning, she thought. Just one more day.

CHAPTER SEVEN

Fanny drove slowly across the bridge in the half-light of early Monday morning, leaving Rowfield sleeping behind her. The strange icon, wrapped in newspaper, was in her weekend bag on the passenger seat.

In spite of what Gaylord had said about the murderer or murderers having already searched her cottage, she was sure they would return to look again. So she took it with her. She'd done a much more careful check than usual to make sure the windows and doors were locked and bolted where possible; she left a note for young Mrs Dean, too, asking her to keep an eye out for strangers. That seemed quite natural after the break-in at Bentham's.

It seemed to Fanny that the answer to the mystery of the strange icon was in London, in the offices of TROD.

Perhaps it was stolen and I can give it back, she said to herself; and if not, I can do a bit of nosing about. She almost added, without Gaylord getting in the way, but she found herself smiling. She had to fight a sudden longing to turn back, to bang on his door until he let her in and then beg him to let her stay with him, she'd learn to cook and she could take the dogs for walks and she'd keep out of his way when he was working. But he doesn't want that, she thought, and nor indeed do I, not really. I'm just nervous about my first day at work. I ought to be looking forward to it, and I am looking forward to it.

But the feeling of depression and foreboding stayed with her. It wasn't helped by the weather. London was grey and dispirited too as she drew up outside the tall, narrow early Victorian terrace house where her flat took up the ground floor and basement. She tripped over a black plastic sack of rubbish someone had left out on the steps. She swore, and then was glad of the evidence of someone else's presence in the house.

Her flat was small, the living room all books and pictures. There were newspapers piled on the table and the seats of the chairs. The gilt mirror above the fireplace was meant to give an illusion of greater space, but merely multiplied the clutter. An arch led to a kitchen, with a large window above the sink looking out on the backs of the identical terrace behind. The window was stifled with leafy potted plants on the shelf behind the sink. There were original shutters on the front window. They'd obviously suffered the same noise problem when the house was built and the traffic was all horse-drawn.

Fanny was proud of the flat. It was her own. Alan had never even been there. She loved the cottage, but it was full of memories, reminders of Alan's betrayal. She hadn't known, when the two of them found it, that already he was seeing Miss America. She suddenly felt a surge of hatred for Alan. He had taken that woman to the cottage. He denied it, but she knew he had. It was two years ago now. She shrugged. She thought maybe the handsome Gaylord Poyntz had driven the ghosts out of it when he jumped into that bed.

But here in London this flat had no ghosts, no past at all.

She changed her clothes. It was almost time to go to work. She was on her way out when the telephone rang.

'It's working again! My telephone. I had to tell you in case you wanted to ring. I hope you like the job. I hope Sir Stafford has recovered from his amnesia or aberration or whatever it was. It seems strange, you know, having someone in London to call. I mean, I don't know anyone to call and chat to. And now there's a beautiful girl.'

They said goodbye. He said good luck. They said goodbye again, and he wished her lots of luck, and then she was out of the door and walking down St John Street with the roof of her mouth beginning to tickle with nerves about her new job, and exactly what would happen when she got to work.

She was certain that someone at TROD must know that poor Mr Burroughs did not die in the car accident as his crisp new death certificate no doubt claimed. And whoever it was knew that she knew too.

CHAPTER EIGHT

The headquarters of Transport, Road and Overseas Development Ltd was a double-fronted Georgian mansion in a cul-de-sac tucked away behind one of the busiest streets in the City of London. One minute Fanny was walking among the latest in trendy towering glass and steel structures, a frantic street with busy stationers and sandwich bars punctuating the stately catalogue of the world's banks, and the next she had stepped into a scene from Dickens, sounds suddenly hushed, hurrying people slowed, a place where it was easier to breathe.

Inside the imposing black double doors of the TROD office, she was conscious of the reverent atmosphere. In the carpeted foyer and on the sweeping shallow stairs everyone seemed to be behaving as though there were someone lying ill in one of the upstairs bedrooms. Telephones didn't ring, they gave a faint burr; the receptionist talked only just above a whisper, and the uniformed security man stood still and silent.

No one had been told to expect Fanny. She had to produce her letter of appointment before another uniformed man was called to escort her up the stairs to the office of Sir Stafford's secretary. Fanny wasn't sure what she'd expected, but Miss Field definitely wasn't it. She was a stout, rather more than middle-aged woman wearing a brown suit which seemed to have been bought many years ago to be timeless. Alan would only have to look at her to make some nasty remark like she looked as though her underwear was bullet-proofed. Miss Field obviously tried to soften the effect with the large flowing bow of a shiny pink blouse. The pink, however, was not kind. Miss Field, Fanny decided, looked as though she should be running a group of Girl Guides in the rural depths of a cold northern county. She was quite out of place in the City of London.

Miss Field seemed to be feeling this herself. She was flustered, explaining to Fanny that she had been on leave taking care of her widowed mother and maiden aunt through a bout of flu when Fanny came to be interviewed, this was her first day back, and she was in what Fanny supposed was a tizz. She was clearly confused that Sir Stafford had appointed Fanny in her absence, but Fanny thought that there was a stern quality about this woman which knew how to deal with nonsense like a little confusion. Her eyes—and her grey hair—might have been cast in steel. Miss Field, everything about her proclaimed, had been with Sir Stafford for years, and would stay with Sir Stafford until she retired to a bungalow in one of the nicest parts of Bournemouth, well away from the summer crowds she would spend much of her time disparaging. Except that Miss Field might not get away to Bournemouth, she seemed to be saddled with her mother and the aunt. 'They should be in a nursing home,' she told Fanny, 'but mother's house in Clapham would have to be sold to pay for that. I don't want that. Mother is used to her own home, and Aunt Emily has lived with her for years. So I pay for daytime nursing, which is a considerable burden, of course. The expense is terrible, and the costs go up all the time, and it's very difficult to find reliable people. That's why I had to take leave. I've got some good people now, but you have to pay for it. Do you have a family?'

'I'm divorced. There weren't any children.'

'I mean a mother or father?'

Fanny said she didn't and Miss Field, for a moment, looked at her as if she had said she had just won the lottery.

Then she returned to fussing about not having been given notice of Fanny's arrival.

She poked her head doubtfully at Fanny. 'Well, I don't know. You'd think he'd at least have left a note. What was the job you were going to do?' She looked as though Fanny had failed to prove her existence.

'*Am*,' Fanny said, '*am* going to do. I am going to run the public relations department.'

'Well, there you are, you see.' Miss Field was triumphant. 'We don't have a public relations department.'

'Quite. That's why I'm here. I'm going to create one.'

Miss Field sighed. She read the letter of appointment again. 'It's a pity Mr Burroughs isn't here, but there you are. What a tragedy!'

Her tone conceded that Fanny was not a presumptuous junior typist.

'A tragedy . . .' Fanny deliberately left it to Miss Field to decide if that was a question or commiseration. Miss Field's mouth clamped shut in what Fanny took to be suppressed reverence for the dead.

'Where is Sir Stafford?' Fanny asked.

Miss Field had obviously been dreading this question. She tried to deflect it by looking affronted, as though Fanny had overstepped some mark of respect in asking it. Fanny waited, and the secretary dropped her pose. It was as though the air had been let out of her.

'I don't know. I don't know where he is or what's happened to him. He's never done such a thing before. I telephoned his home—his London home—and he had not returned from the weekend. But when I contacted his place in the country, they said he's in London.'

'But he was driving the car when Mr Burroughs was killed,' Fanny said. 'Didn't you know that?'

Miss Field looked as though Fanny had kicked her.

'No!' she said. 'Oh, no. How do *you* know that?'

'I just happen to have a place in Oxfordshire near where it happened.'

'But Sir Stafford's home is in Gloucestershire.' Miss Field looked as though she was about to swoon.

Fanny glanced round for the inevitable kettle. It stood on a silver tray on the broad window ledge, with a neat stack of teabags, a jar of instant coffee, and an unopened carton of milk beside a silver jug. The kettle was full. Fanny turned it on.

'We'll have tea,' she said. 'We've both had shocks.'

Even if it meant hearing more about Mother and Aunt Emily in the house in Clapham, Fanny thought it best to be kind to Miss Field.

'What a terrible morning,' Miss Field said, holding her head in her hands. 'Mr Burroughs dead and Sir Stafford—'

Fanny put a cup of tea in front of her. 'Drink it,' she said. 'You'll feel better.'

Miss Field sipped the tea. She smiled at Fanny. 'It's not right,' she said. 'They were close at work, of course, but Sir Stafford isn't a man to mix socially with the staff, you know, outside the office. Mr Burroughs would never have been in the car with him at a weekend.'

She put down the cup and took a deep breath. 'Do you know what happened to Sir Stafford after the accident?'

'You mean what's the local gossip?' Fanny said. 'The police say he ran off and disappeared. They know it was him because someone saw him. Besides, his wallet was in the car.'

Miss Field flushed a deep, dark red. 'No!'

she said in protest, 'never. Sir Stafford would never do anything . . . dishonourable. Ran off? Disappeared? Oh, no, out of the question.'

Fanny said nothing. There was nothing she could say. She knew Mr Burroughs had not been killed in the crash, but the police were sure about Sir Stafford. There was his wallet, and the other driver had identified him.

'I don't know what we're going to do with you, you know,' Miss Field said.

'I shall start a public relations department,' Fanny said. 'We may need one, if the press get to hear of Sir Stafford's disappearance.'

'But—'

Fanny cut across what was certainly going to be a catalogue of reasons why she should go away and become someone else's problem. 'I shall use Mr Burroughs' office,' she said.

Miss Field looked shocked. 'Oh, no, really! I don't think that's very proper, do you?' Her mouth puckered.

'Yes, perfectly,' Fanny said. 'It's the best solution. We know Mr Burroughs won't be needing it.' Fanny felt she had to startle Miss Field out of her assumption of authority. 'Please don't worry about me. You must have a lot to catch up on, if you've been away. I know which room it is. I was there on Friday. Remember, the name is Fanny Dinmont, Mrs Dinmont. Perhaps you will let the switchboard know.'

Fanny took her cup of tea to Mr Burroughs'

office. It was a large, well-proportioned room, painted a pale green which made it seem colder than it was. There was a large wooden desk, a couple of leather chairs and a bookshelf. A computer under a plastic cover stood on a table in the corner. Fanny could see it was not plugged into the socket in the wall. The room was theatrically masculine in an old-fashioned way, it smelled of wood polish and tobacco. There was a rack of pipes on the mantle of a pale grey, mottled marble fireplace.

Fanny sat at Mr Burroughs' desk in Mr Burroughs' chair. She looked about her, wondering what the room could tell her about why he was killed. The desk top was empty, without even a photograph, not even a formal pen-holder or a sheet of blotting paper. Nothing. To her right the handsome bookcase held heavy tomes on international law and other reference works, a current *Who's Who,* and last year's *Who Owns Whom.* There were a few paperback editions of American books on man management tucked into a corner. Perhaps after all Mr Burroughs had been ambitious.

Fanny got up and walked across to the window. A casement, floor-length, it opened on to a narrow balcony where someone had tried to encourage a tired fuschia to flower. Fanny leaned forward and stared down into the street. There were cars and pedestrians, but the cul-de-sac still gave an impression of being removed from time. Two or three dark-suited men with briefcases hurried towards the offices in the terrace of narrow houses at the end. Except for an absence of bowlers, and absolutely no top hats, Fanny thought, Dickens would be quite at home.

She wondered if Mr Burroughs had broken off in the mornings to come and look down on this quiet corner of the teeming City, his mind on other things as he watched the world go by. What had he thought about as he stared out? Fishing a dappled river, or his own echoing footsteps among deserted ruins in the Peloponnese; or perhaps the sweet scent of old-fashioned roses in his own back garden in his Southern Region suburb?

In any case he had left no clues in this detached, cool room where the furniture and the dark-framed pictures of murky landscapes on the walls looked as if they were on loan from a gentlemen's club. Mr Burroughs might never have existed as far as this impersonal office was concerned. And now he didn't exist, he had lain dead on her living-room floor, and he hadn't risen from the dead to die in Sir Stafford Williams' car. Somebody had moved him, and that somebody was more likely than not to be here at TROD.

CHAPTER NINE

The door of the office burst open. Fanny jumped up as though to defend herself. Why am I behaving as though I'm guilty of something? she asked herself, and sat down again to glare at the man who had come into the room.

He was a tall man, large but not fat, with pale brown hair cut short. He looked like someone who had been to an army barber and was now trying to grow it out. He stared at her in an astonished way.

'What are you doing here?' he demanded. The voice went with the haircut, it was an army officer's voice.

'If you are not going to introduce yourself, and if you're entitled to know, I expect Sir Stafford's secretary will tell you. Do you normally burst into people's offices without knocking?'

He stared at her like a goldfish that had been given the power of speech but could think of nothing to say. Fanny had to force herself to meet his grey, moonstone eyes in case she started to laugh. He looked ridiculous.

'I am entitled to know what you're doing in this office, you know,' he said. 'I am entitled to come into any room in this building I want without knocking. Certainly any room where you are likely to be.' He spoke in a tone of outraged injury.

'Any room?' Fanny asked. 'Does that include the ladies'?' Of course, you know, even if you're maintenance, you ought at least to knock . . . in case a girl is powdering her nose.'

'What? Maintenance? You think I could be . . . Good God, I'm Mr Ramsey.' Fury made him sweat. His broad face began to glisten. 'I am Ian Ramsey, Sir Stafford's deputy. I run the company in his absence. If you work here, I am your boss. And if you do work here, I'm going to find out why, and make sure you won't be working here any longer.'

'Oh, so you're Ian Ramsey?' Fanny said. 'Sir Stafford told me about you. He said I'd like you, that we'd get along together. I suppose even Sir Stafford can't be right all the time.'

Ian Ramsey loomed a moment longer in the doorway. Fanny was glad she was sitting behind the broad-topped desk. He looked angry enough to hit her. Then he laughed. 'Christ,' he said, 'you can't possibly be the new public relations person, or can you?'

He moved into the room, shutting the door behind him. He was not angry any more. 'I suppose you'll be a bit more polite to the public when you're relating to them.'

'As long as the public knocks before it enters,' she said. She held out her hand. 'My name is Fanny Dinmont. I took this office because it's not being used, for obvious reasons. You startled me, I'm afraid. I must say, though, I can see why Sir Stafford thinks the company needs a new image if all the top personnel are as aggressive as you.'

'Dinmont? You can't be Alan's ex, can you?'

'You know Alan?'

'In the line of business, and golf. It was I who suggested you to Sir Stafford. Alan had mentioned you, and when Sir Stafford said he was looking . . . I thought of you.'

'Thank you.'

Ramsey smiled. He was quite good-looking now that he was being friendly. Fanny tried to imagine him on the golf links with Alan. She couldn't. Alan hadn't been a golfer when she knew him.

'Well,' he said, 'things are a bit on edge this morning.' He smiled again, apparently sympathetic and appeasing. 'You were, as you know, hired personally by Sir Stafford.'

He makes me seem like Sir Stafford's little indiscretion, Fanny thought. But the Ramsey smile became a grin.

'You know,' he said, 'I think it might be best all round if, until he returns, you delay actually coming to the office. We'll pay you, of course, but I really can't see how you can be usefully employed until Sir Stafford returns to make use of whatever talent he feels you . . . after all, he employed you, so only he knows exactly what he had in mind for you to do.'

Now Fanny laughed. 'I would imagine Sir Stafford's absence in itself will bring me quite enough work to keep me busy.'

'Are you suggesting, Mrs Dinmont, that Sir Stafford intended you to stand in for him?'

Fanny sighed. She thought she'd better explain as clearly and firmly as she could the position the company was in.

'You seem to miss the point, Mr Ramsey. Sir Stafford hasn't got flu. He has disappeared. I understand the police are looking for him. You can't keep it quiet. He must have appointments to keep. He's due somewhere and he won't turn up. Questions will be asked. It won't be long before the press are all over the place looking for clues and reasons, and speculating all sorts of things which could do the company a great deal of harm here and overseas. There'll surely be an effect on the money markets. It will come out that the police want to question him; that he was last seen disappearing from a fatal car crash. It'll be big news. I would be happy to leave you to deal with it, but it is the sort of thing Sir Stafford hired me to do. It won't be a bit of good you telling the press you've nothing to say. You can repeat that as many times and as loudly as you like but the press will crucify you, and Sir Stafford, and this company.'

Fanny got up and slowly and calmly began to search her handbag for car keys. She smiled very sweetly at Mr Ramsey. He looked worried and was stroking his chin thoughtfully with one hand.

'I detect the note of relish in your voice,' he said. 'I suppose it's a sign that you love your work. You think it'll get in the papers, then? That Sir Stafford has really disappeared?'

'Of course it will. How can you imagine it wouldn't? It's a great story.' Fanny sounded cheerful. 'Good thing, too, if you ask me. The press will keep the police up to the mark. I'm surprised they haven't been on to you already.'

'No, we can't have that,' Ian Ramsey said. He looked more than worried now, almost frightened. 'We can't risk losing confidence abroad. It'll do terrible damage to the company—to the country, even. Thousands of people depend on the good name of TROD. We can't risk that. What do we do?'

It's probably a bit late now,' she said, 'but if I were you, I'd hire a public relations person. At least then you could control the information given out.'

He smiled. This time it was a smile of capitulation and appeal. 'You win,' he said. 'What do we do now?'

Fanny sat down again at Mr Burroughs' desk.

'It's not going to be easy. We'll have to try to divert the press somehow. We can't hide the fact that Sir Stafford has disappeared, what we've got to avoid is giving away the real situation.'

'Sure, sure,' Ian Ramsey said. He drummed his fingers on the top of the desk. 'Lie, you mean. What's our story then?'

'No, not lie. We've got to help them jump to the wrong conclusion. We tell them Sir Stafford's taking a few days off to recover after a car crash, not that he's run off from a fatal accident to avoid the consequences.'

'But won't the police release the details?'

'Not unless they're asked?'

'The chief constable's a friend of Sir Stafford's.'

'That's up to you,' Fanny said. 'I just deal with the questions as they come.'

And how will you do that?'

Fanny didn't want to tell him she didn't know, and that she saw very little chance of success whatever she did. But he was waiting for an answer. She shrugged.

'The best way I know to put off the press is to give them a story about good works. Somehow we've got to get in first. We could put out a release that Sir Stafford was about to announce plans to do something worthy, but all that's been delayed by his accident. At least if they believe he was on his way to some sort of good works, he wasn't likely to be drunk. It had better be some project to help young people in some Third World country. If the papers get nasty they'll look as though they're hounding a Nice Person. Then you say he's had a car crash in which his old friend was killed and the matter *is sub judice,* and with any luck at all they'll drop it.'

'Isn't it *sub judice?'*

'Don't think so. No one's been charged. Don't worry. We'll bore them off the telephone.'

'What a strange calling you have,' Ian Ramsey said. 'It's shock, of course. Sir Stafford, I mean. A man of his age in a car crash like that. Poor old Burroughs dead beside him, of course he'd go into shock. He's probably lost his memory. The police will understand that.'

Fanny thought of Inspector Fulwell, Sergeant Kerslake, and Constable Mimms. 'Will they?' she said.

'The chief constable will,' Ian Ramsey said. He smiled and again she thought he was good-looking. She could see him teeing off and putting on a green, being pleasant to all sorts of unlikeable people because Ian Ramsey was a pleasant man. She had got off to a bad start with him when he burst through her door, but she thought they would get along now.

Fanny settled down to write a rough draft of a press release. I'd better get Ian Ramsey's approval, she thought. No point in antagonising him more than I have already.

So later that morning she went to ask Miss Field which was his office.

'Is everything all right for you?' Sir Stafford's secretary asked. 'You'll have to forgive the way things are today, it's not usually like this. Usually everyone's so nice. Mr Ramsey is a very nice young man. He always stops and talks to me about his golf game. I don't know a thing about golf, but he loves to tell me about his rounds on the links.'

So she heard my little opening contretemps with Ian Ramsey, Fanny thought. Is she putting me in my place, or showing female solidarity?

Ramsey's office was a complete contrast to the displaced gentlemen's club smoking room of Mr Burroughs. It reminded Fanny of a science laboratory, cool and white and a lot of polished metal. Very clinical and focused. Where Mr Burroughs was the old guard, Ian Ramsey proclaimed himself the new blood in the firm.

He motioned Fanny to sit down. 'I've something to show you,' he said.

He took a folded piece of paper from the inside pocket of his jacket, which was hanging on the back of a tubular steel chair. 'Look,' he said, 'I've received this.'

Fanny unfolded it. It was a note in the jittery script of a man used only to signing his name, not writing to communicate. It was signed Stafford Williams.

Ian Ramsey took it back before Fanny could read it properly.

'I imagine this settles it,' he said. 'Or at least, it clears up the mystery. It says he's gone off to think for a while. Shocked about the car crash—just as I said—and we mustn't worry about him. He puts the firm in what he calls "my capable hands" till he returns. He wants to rethink a few things.'

'Sir Stafford said that—that he wants to *rethink* things?'

'Well, that's what it amounts to. He's obviously feeling bad about Burroughs.'

'When did it come?'

'Earlier this morning. Miss Field brought it in.'

Fanny thought of the Sir Stafford she had met in his office on the top floor just three days ago. He didn't strike her then as the kind of man who would write scrappy notes about having to think things over.

But Ramsey was satisfied. He was even pleased. The winning smile was on show again, but this time Fanny didn't think it made him good-looking. It made him look smug.

'What about the police?' she asked.

'Oh, that's not such a bad outlook as you might have thought. The lorry driver has told them it wasn't Sir Stafford's fault.'

'That's a most accommodating lorry driver! A real Knight of the Road. And what about the cops? They being jolly good sorts as well?'

'I'm told that Sir Stafford's sent them a signed statement.'

'Surely that's not enough. Not with a fatality. Not even with a billion pounds and a fatality.'

'What a cynic you are! And you look quite the opposite, so sweet and gentle.' Ramsey smiled to show he admired her appearance, and didn't take the cynicism too seriously.

'Where did Sir Stafford's letter come from?'

'Come from? From Sir Stafford, of course. I told you, Miss Field . . .'

'No, the postmark on the envelope. Where was it posted?'

Ramsey glanced at the letter in his hands. 'I never thought to look. It came in a pile Miss Field brought in.' He began to rummage in a waste-paper basket. 'I think it was delivered by hand. Had "personal" on it, addressed to me.' He was still bent over looking through the basket.

'Here it is.'

He held up the envelope for her to see. There was no stamp. 'You see, I told you, it came by hand. Have a drink, Fanny. You deserve it after the sterling work you've put in this morning.'

He straightened and moved across the room to a small bar against the wall.

Fanny turned. A flash of colour on the wall near the bar caught her eye—rich red, ochre, gold and green. She caught her breath. On Ian Ramsey's office wall, not prominently displayed, but clearly within his line of vision from his seat at his glass-topped desk, hung a large, glowing icon.

It's like the other one, Fanny thought. It could be made by the same man.

'It's beautiful!' she said.

Ian Ramsey followed her gaze. He showed no interest.

'Is it?' he said. 'It's just something that hangs on the wall. I suppose it came from the art pool when the office was redecorated for me. It's a bit primitive, that sort of thing, if you ask me. Now these . . .' He had a surprisingly strong grasp as he took her elbow and moved her away towards a set of golfing prints hanging together near the door. 'These are what I call real art . . .'

He was smiling, being pleasant, with his jokey air of the philistine.

Could the glowing icon on the wall be coincidence? Surely not. And Fanny didn't for a moment believe that letter from Sir Stafford. She didn't know Sir Stafford's handwriting, she really didn't know Sir Stafford, but there was something phoney about the set up which she didn't like.

CHAPTER TEN

Newspaper reporters rang at intervals throughout the afternoon. They were going through the motions, hoping for some kind of scandal behind the non-committal wording of the statement Fanny had released through the Press Association. It was not difficult to deflect them. Sir Stafford Williams was too old for a sex scandal, too Establishment for drugs or corruption. Though he was powerful, his power was not evident. He was no dynastic mogul; outside the City pages his name was unknown. The popular newspapers decided he was not the stuff of news; the quality papers awaited whatever financial consequences might arise to tempt their interest. Some, she supposed, were wondering whether they had better update the obituary they kept in stock.

As Fanny dealt with the calls which confirmed Sir Stafford as a shadowy creature as alien from the interests of ordinary people as an owl from sparrows, she found she was becoming curious about him.

Some of the reporters tried her out with anecdotes which might strike a confidence from her. Stories of his meanness, his greed, his misogyny, stories in which the reporters lacked conviction as they told them. Fanny sounded regretful as she denied them, conveying to the pressured faceless newshounds that she wished Sir Stafford could be as interesting as they were trying to make him. But where the reporters lost interest, Fanny found she wanted to know more.

She tried to remember exactly what he looked like, but could only conjure up an impression of dark suit, sallow, wrinkled skin, and very carefully manicured hands.

He was a man of enormous power, she knew that, but he appeared to have no interest in using it politically; a man of achievement for which he sought no public recognition; a vain man, dressed as a tribute to traditional craftsmen, yet he seemed to have no concern for the admiration of women. Nor for men.

Who's Who whetted her appetite. Sir Stafford, it seemed, had attended no school or university. He had never married. He did absolutely nothing with his time outside the company. He acknowledged no interests sporting, literary or recreational. He gave his address as the London offices of TROD.

She stopped thinking of Sir Stafford and thought of Gaylord Poyntz. She had no trouble visualising Gaylord, with his tweed suit that looked home made, the sort of tweeds that only Americans wore nowadays, his tall, slightly stooping frame; and the tortoiseshell rimmed half-glasses that he wore to read and, presumably, to draw his cartoons. He was a man who looked as though he were playing a part, from his black felt hat to the tip of his gleaming brown full-brogue shoes.

And if he's playing a part, she thought, now his role includes being my lover.

That made her happy, but she wished she knew a bit more about him.

She had no way of checking up on American cartoonists. But she had the reference books right there in the office to find out something about Gaylord's friend Harry. That might make her feel she was getting closer to Gaylord himself.

She felt guilty as she looked up Harry Hughes's name. But she needn't have bothered, he wasn't in *Who's Who,* he wasn't in any of the books, and yet he was obviously rich and successful. She had been in his house, she had seen the pictures and the furniture, and the vintage American Buick. His money must come from somewhere outside the financial and industrial mainstream. Maybe he had inherited it—or he could be a crook. Gaylord didn't look like the sort of man who would look for references about what his friends and acquaintances did for a living.

Who's talking? Fanny asked herself. She didn't like to admit it, but she wouldn't be able to swear that her ex-husband Alan wasn't prepared to cut a few corners if he was sure he wouldn't be found out.

The telephone rang once more. She picked it up and Gaylord's growling voice started singing to her

'You *say icon and I say eecon,*
Icon, eecon, let's call the whole thing off

I haven't written any more. It's a beautiful day down here, very warm, and I'm sitting in Harry's study with a whisky, and I thought of you.'

'That's nice,' Fanny said. 'In very different circumstances I was just thinking of you. Do you really need glasses to read?'

'Wait a minute, I'll see . . . No, no I don't. They're a harmless affectation to make me look like a kindly old cartoonist. Everyone my age needs glasses to read. You will, too. How's tricks? Keeping track of the bodies Lost and Found? Better lost than found, this weather.'

'You're the pits, Poyntz. It's been quite a day here.'

She was going to ask him right out what Harry Hughes did to get so rich, but he might detect and misunderstand the element of suspicion in the question and she thought she'd wait for another time.

Gaylord said, 'You sound awful. Like one of those dreadful young women who walk round with briefcases and coloured stockings and wear spectacles to make themselves look like they can read. Why don't you ask me what I'm wearing at this moment?'

'Spats?' Fanny said. 'You are a young man in spats.'

She had not noticed anyone come into her office. She raised her head and saw Ian Ramsey standing in front of her. He was smiling.

'I can't tell you any more, I'm afraid,' she said into the receiver. She put the phone down on Gaylord's mocking laughter.

Damn, she thought, how long has he been listening? 'Another reporter,' she said, and added, 'one I used to know.'

'I would have knocked, but the door was open.'

'What can I do for you?'

'I want to thank you, that's all. For all you've done today. I hoped you'd spare me a moment to have a drink before you go so we could have a chat about where we go from here?'

Fanny was about to refuse, but then she thought of the mysterious icon on Ramsey's office wall.

'Thanks,' she said, giving him a big bright silly smile, the smile of a girl who chats with her boyfriend on the office phone. 'I could do with one.'

She caught him give her a speculative glance. Did he suspect her? What of? No, she said to herself, Ian Ramsey is a man who takes it for granted women find him attractive. He's weighing up his chances.

In his office he poured the glass of Campari she thought was the kind of drink he would expect her to choose.

'Well,' he said, sitting beside her on a large leather settee, 'any further developments?'

'It's not easy answering questions about someone you don't know,' she said. 'I mean, what's Sir Stafford really like?'

The simplistic question seemed to put him at ease. He stretched out his very solid legs and leaned back against the cushions.

'I sometimes wonder if he's interested in the business for its own sake at all,' he said. 'Money's what it's all about, of course.'

'Money may be part of it,' she said, 'but there must be more to it than that. What does the company do?' Wide-eyed, Fanny thought, look wide-eyed, dumb, impressed.

She thought he was going to chuck her under the chin like a little girl but if so, he thought better of it. Instead he smiled kindly at her.

'All sorts of things to do with money,' he said. 'International trade, that kind of thing. It comes down to making money work. Sir Stafford's very interested in Third World Development, actually. And he's very generous in that area. But you knew that.'

'Yes,' Fanny said. 'You told me. And Mr Burroughs did as well.'

'Ah,' Ramsey said, 'poor old Bill.'

'What about you? What are you interested in? You sound as if you think Sir Stafford's personal interests are rather bad for the business.'

'Now, now,' he said, in a teasing voice, 'scratch a single-minded career woman and there's always a woolly liberal under the wolf's clothing. No, it can be good for business. Good PR, which you'll appreciate. It just doesn't interest me particularly, that's all.'

'So what particular aspect of big business is

your passion?' She was deliberately arch.

'Me?' he said, 'I'm one of those very boring businessmen who really is a company man.'

'Oh, no, let me guess. What interests you? Not icons, apparently; nor good works. Politics? No, perhaps not. Sport?'

'Well, there's my golf. But why not politics?'

'I don't see you on committees and sucking up to selection panels. You don't strike me as someone who works as part of a group, more a man of action. I'd put you down as a bit of a loner. You know, like the Elizabethan pirates of old, like Drake, or Raleigh.' Steady on, she told herself. Flattery may get you anywhere, but there's a point even his vanity won't swallow this stuff.

'There's no mystery about me,' he said. 'Work, a round or two of golf at weekends, more work. What about you? What's your interest in icons and the labyrinthine TROD?'

He got up to refill their glasses as he asked the question. His tone was teasing. But Fanny thought she sensed a change in the atmosphere. Be careful what you say to him, she said to herself.

'I was just making conversation,' she said. 'I needed a job, but you know Alan, you know about that. I'm incredibly grateful. This job is a way of paying the mortgage. Ex-journalists really aren't qualified for much, you know.'

'An ex-journalist, eh? They do say once a journalist, always a journalist. What kind of journalist?'

'Well, there you are, you see, I probably wasn't really what you'd call a journalist at all. Just women's stuff, you know.' It sounded as feeble as she had intended. She wondered what Alan had told him about her. Probably only the usual ex-husband stuff, that she was a hard-faced bitch.

'And icons?' Ramsey asked. 'Do you collect them?'

Fanny was going to tell him about her own modest collection, but she stopped herself. For a man who professed no interest in icons, he was harping on the subject.

'Oh, that! It's just that it caught my eye. The colours are so lovely. The red and green is just what I want for my sitting room curtains, but I can't find anything I like.'

There, she thought, that's womansy enough for him. He said, 'Yes, I suppose it is pretty, if you like that kind of thing. I'm more interested in art as an investment. For me that's the point.'

'How do you mean?' Fanny opened her eyes in apparent wonder over the rim of her drink.

'The point? Oh, if I owned something it would be because other people would pay a lot of money for it,' he said. He leaned towards her and smiled. 'Now I know that you covet the thing for your sitting-room colour scheme, I'll treasure it more.'

Fanny, smiling, got up and walked across

the room to study the icon. The face of the saint glowed, his dark eyes were hypnotic. The lettered scroll he held was grasped in unnaturally big hands.

'I like it,' she said. 'Is it valuable?'

'Oh, it'll be the real thing. Would you like it? I'll lend it to you. You can put it in old Bill's . . . in your office. It'll cheer up those dark landscapes he had on the walls.'

'Oh, I don't think so, I'd be afraid to have anything valuable like that. Thank you, but—'

'Nothing is valuable until other people want it.'

He took the icon down from the wall and handed it to her. She held it, feeling the age of the wood under her fingers.

'Is it Greek, do you think?' she asked. 'They're usually Greek, aren't they?'

'Or Russian. But this icon is Ethiopian, and very rare indeed.' And if you weren't interested in icons, you couldn't possibly know that, Fanny thought.

He was watching her. The pleasant smile had faded. She was suddenly cold, feeling those pale grey blank eyes on her. There was something spooky about those eyes. What a cliche, the villain with the staring eyes, the hypnotic glare of the murderer! God, even Miss Field's eyes sometimes gleamed like cold steel. Even so, there was something about Ian Ramsey that made her afraid of him.

CHAPTER ELEVEN

It was nearly nine when she left the office to walk home. Ian Ramsey's comments about the value of things kept coming into her mind. What must it be like to see everything in terms of the value other people put on it? Poor Ian! Probably not a villain at all, just a great golf bore.

Once back at the flat she rang Gaylord.

'Why, if it isn't Fanny Dinmont,' he said. 'Found any bodies?'

'I haven't even found a skeleton in a cupboard,' she said. 'But I'll work on it. What about your end?'

'What am I working on? Whisky.'

'Nothing new there then? But don't be daft, you're holding out on me. Something's happened.'

She heard the clink of his signet ring against glass. She listened to him swallow.

'Well, it could be nothing,' he said at last. 'But it seems the only thing stolen in the Bentham's break-in was one of a pair of very rare Georgian candlesticks. Brass, in very good condition, and *valuable.* And guess what? I went down to look at the survivor on the pretext of . . . I forget what my pretext was, as a matter of fact . . .'

'Get on with it,' Fanny said.

'Oh, yes, the survivor. It's a dead ringer for the murder weapon which is stashed away in your bushes and not in such good condition. What do you make of that?'

Fanny hesitated. She was sorry to throw damp water on his enthusiasm. 'Well,' she said, 'not a lot at the moment. But it does mean the murder and the break-in are connected. Do you think poor old Mr Burroughs stole it?'

'Have *you* been drinking?' Gaylord asked. 'He'd have taken both of them. They're not worth much apart. Like swans, they mate for life. Speaking of which, I've decided I'm missing you.'

'You *are* drunk!' She imagined him standing at the telephone in his paper-strewn study with the door open, the shadows swaying a little in the light of the chandelier on the landing. Outside the uncurtained window the village would already have pulled a blanket over its head and settled for the night. She hoped he would cook something for his supper, then stopped herself short. How ridiculous! 'Oh, iron your own shirts,' she said aloud.

He burst out laughing. 'You bet I will,' he said. 'I wouldn't let one of you drip-dry women near my authentic items. I've told you my news. Have you got anything to tell me?'

'Nothing. Nothing at all. It's like everyone's walking on tiptoe. They're all hidden away behind beautiful original Georgian doors with not a blot or a dropped ballpoint or a screwed up piece of paper to be seen.'

'You're used to newspaper offices, perhaps that's what seems odd? How did they cope with no Sir Stafford Williams? Panic?'

'Ian Ramsey, his deputy, seemed to think it was quite natural.'

'That's interesting.'

'Is it?'

'Have you done anything about the icon?'

Fanny glanced automatically at the bookshelf where she had pushed it, still wrapped in newspaper, behind a set of Jane Austen. The newspaper was the Rowfield free sheet. She wished she was back in the village now, in her own cottage, or even sipping whisky, with Gaylord sagging in his armchair.

Gaylord said:

'There's a man I did a job for once, he'd tell you about it. He works for one of the auction houses, but if you mention my name he'll look at it for you. His name's Parfitt. Hang on.'

Fanny waited. She could hear him rifling through papers, swearing to himself. Then he came back on the line and recited a telephone number.

'Percy Parfitt sounds perfect,' she said. 'I'll ring him tomorrow.'

When she put down the phone she remembered that she still hadn't asked him where Harry Hughes got his money.

CHAPTER TWELVE

She had expected to spot Percy Parfitt right away. Gaylord had described him as a typical icon expert. She stood at the bar of the pub where she'd arranged to meet him with the icon in her shopping bag and scanned the faces of the men around her. They looked identical to her. No one stood out. But I do, she thought, there's not another woman on her own in the place.

A well-dressed middle-aged man approached her. There was the hint of a question in his smile. My God, she thought, he's going to try to pick me up.

'I'm waiting for someone,' she said, before he could speak. He had the type of distinguished, hawk-nosed looks Fanny liked.

'Me, I hope,' he said. 'Are you Fanny? I'm Percy Parfitt.'

She knew she must have looked surprised because he said, 'What were you expecting? What kind of weirdo did Gaylord make me out to be?'

Fanny laughed and shook his hand.

They sat at a table in a corner protected from the crush of people by a pillar. She held the icon on her knees under the table while he ordered a bottle of St Emilion and smoked salmon sandwiches. Then he leaned across the table.

'You've got something to show me?'

She noticed his beautifully manicured hands as he unwrapped the newspaper and took out the icon.

She heard him catch his breath. His face had a rapt expression. This was love. For a fleeting moment Fanny felt sad that no one would ever look at her like that; Alan never had, and Gaylord had surely never looked at any girl like that. If he ever did, she thought, he's much too old now.

'It's wonderful,' Percy Parfitt said. His voice shook a little, as though he was suffering from shock. He rewrapped the icon in the rumpled Rowfield free sheet. He looks frightened, Fanny thought, and then she wondered, is that what awe looks like?

She was disappointed that he seemed to want to hide the icon, not talk about it.

'Can't you tell me anything about it?' she said.

'I can't study it here,' he said. 'I thought . . . well, I never dreamed . . . My God, you mean you brought it here like that on the *bus?*'

'What's the matter?' she asked. 'You look as if you've seen a ghost. Do you know something about it? Is it some well-known piece stolen from a museum or something?'

Parfitt drained his glass before he answered. 'You must understand that I may be quite wrong. It may be a clever fake, or nothing at all.' He stopped and shook his head.

'Well?' Fanny said, 'tell me what you think?'

'To be frank, I can't believe I can be right. It can't be true, but it seems to me that it might be a Crusader icon.'

'A Crusader icon? What's that?'

'We know so little about them,' Percy Parfitt said. 'In fact, practically all the study so far has been based on the icons discovered in a monastery on an expedition in 1965. That's when we discovered the work of Latin artists in the Crusader Kingdom.'

'You mean the Christians brought icons with them and left them in the monasteries they set up?'

'No, more than that. At first that's what we'd thought, that they were gifts, but now it seems that individual painters worked out there and set up workshops with pupils to produce a distinct body of work.'

'My God,' Fanny said, looking in awe at the package on the table between them. 'How old does that make it?'

Parfitt took a deep breath. 'Twelfth or thirteenth century,' he said. He tried to sound matter of fact, but his voice rose to end in a squeak of excitement. 'The Crusader icons were mostly made by French and Italian artists working over there. This looks French to me, with those rolling eyes. Very typical, I believe.'

He pulled a corner of the newspaper wrapping back and pointed to the background of the second row of saints.

'You see?' he said in a reverential whisper, 'you see that? Those lances with pennants showing a red cross on white ground.' Then, as though he had been caught doing something forbidden, he put the paper back. 'Did you see?'

It had looked like a blur to Fanny. She shook her head.

'It's out of my league,' she said. 'I've just got a few nineteenth century icons because I like them. But why . . . what makes it look so different from an icon a Frenchman working in France might have painted?'

'It's the style. The Western artists working in the East were surrounded by genuine Byzantine art. They imitated it; they became part of it. Back at home, though, the Byzantine influence was absorbed in what the Renaissance critics called *maniera bizantina,* they copied a style in the manner of . . .'

'So why do you think these Crusader icons were painted by Europeans in the Middle East? Why not by locals on the spot?'

'There again,' Parfitt said, 'most of them had developed their own western style before they went. They didn't lose that. The way they showed the human body, for instance. There's a Western realism there. These Crusader icons are an early link between Eastern and Western painting.'

Parfitt stopped talking, and they drank in

silence for a while.

'Sorry,' he said, 'I have to lecture you like a text book or I just might get up and dance on the tables making awful noises and frightening the natives. I can't believe this is happening. And it may not be, you know. I could be quite wrong.'

Fanny thought he gave her a rather odd look.

'It isn't mine,' she said. 'Gaylord told you that?'

'He said you found it.'

Percy Parfitt smiled to show that he wasn't going to ask questions, but that he thought Gaylord should think up a better cover story.

'Yes,' said Fanny, 'I did.' She told him how the icon had come into her possession. 'So,' she said when she finished, 'what do you make of that?'

He spread his beautifully kept hands. 'Beats me,' he said. He looked at the wrapped icon on the table. 'It's sad, isn't it? A wonderful work of art like this, and it can only be here because of some sort of skulduggery. Murder and money!'

'What is it worth? Can you guess?'

Parfitt sighed. 'It's always the same question,' he said. He shook his head. 'It's priceless. There's nothing to compare it with. Quite priceless.' He hesitated, then spoke in a nervous, urgent tone. 'Fanny, this company, TROD? Where do they operate?'

'Everywhere. A genuine multinational. But Sir Stafford Williams at least has special interest in developing countries, in Africa and Asia.'

'You see, as far as we know the Crusader icons that survived the heathen hordes were hidden in monasteries like St Catherine's at Sinai. There's been very little study, because there's not much to study, but we've always known it's possible there were workshops making icons in countries bordering the old Crusader kingdom.'

Fanny began to realize the implications of what he was saying. 'You mean someone's found one of those work-shops?'

'It's just a thought. This may simply be a magnificent one-off with a provenance going back centuries in the same family. But—'

'But it isn't a one-off,' Fanny said. Parfitt had to lean forward to hear her. 'I know where there's another like it,' she whispered.

He stared at her, shocked.

'Another one?' he said.

'It's actually hanging on the wall in my office at TROD. Mr Ramsey let me have it.'

'Mr Ramsey?'

'It was on his wall before mine, but he's into very modern decor and he didn't think it went with chrome and executive toys. He insisted I take it. He can't think it's worth anything.'

'Fanny, be careful.'

'Don't tell me to go to the police, because

for various reasons I can't. What about this icon?'

'Well, for various reasons I won't tell you to go to the police. I want to make a few inquiries of my own. A beautiful thing like this brings out the worst in us all, I'm afraid. Money for some, possession for others—for me, I can't resist a kind of scholastic megalomania. It's the chance of a place in history.'

'Worth killing for?'

'It's enough that it exists.'

'If it were mine to give, I'd give it to you,' Fanny said.

He smiled at her, then picked up the package, ready to leave. 'Oh, no,' he said, 'if this is what I think it is, it belongs to everyone. But it's never as simple as that. Think what's been done in the name of some of the great diamonds.'

Fanny had no idea what trouble great diamonds had caused, except that in old-fashioned murder mysteries people were killed for them.

She said, 'But this is a religious symbol. It's not the same.'

'Icons have caused chaos before. In the eighth century the reaction against making representations of Christ nearly brought down the Byzantine civilization.'

Fanny stood up to go. 'Thank you,' she said. 'Keep me posted. I hope we can meet and have a proper talk about icons one day.'

Percy Parfitt held on to the hand she extended. 'You know, I heard a story the other day, a story about Ethiopia. I was told that since the Marxist coup some of the priests have been copying their religious works of art. Then they sell off the real thing and put the copies in the churches. What do you think of that?'

'Sell them off? Who do they sell them to?'

'That's the question, isn't it? We should keep that in mind.'

He tucked the newspaper more closely round the icon. He stopped. 'Now this is a coincidence,' he said. 'The *Rowfield Newsletter.* That's Rowfield-on-Thames, isn't it?'

'Yes,' Fanny said, 'I—'

'Now this is curious,' he said. 'I told you there's very little known about the icon trade, but if there's one man who might have a few ideas, he comes from Rowfield-on-Thames. His name's Scruton, Piers Scruton. Works for Bentham's, the antique dealers.'

'That's extraordinary,' Fanny said. 'I know Bentham's.'

'Haven't seen the fellow for years, mind you. He may have moved on to something less rarefied.'

'I've never seen an icon in Bentham's.'

'Odd how this one turned up on Piers' doorstep, isn't it?' mused Percy Parfitt.

As she was going out he caught up with her and said:

'Keep your eyes and ears open, Fanny, but be careful. I wouldn't ask too many questions if I were you.'

CHAPTER THIRTEEN

Miss Field was becoming daily more stiff-backed and tight-lipped. Fanny reminded herself how worried the poor woman was about taking care of her mother and her aunt without selling the family home in Clapham. In addition, there was the gloom that had descended on the TROD office in the wake of Mr Burroughs' death and the continuing absence of Sir Stafford Williams. Fanny imagined that Miss Field was cracking up.

She tried to be especially nice to her. But this seemed to make Miss Field even more remote.

Something had to be done, though, to ease Miss Field's anxiety. On Friday morning Fanny called Miss Field to her office. The secretary came in, shorthand notebook at the ready. She was wearing the same suit as the day Fanny first saw her, but a Peter Pan collar now replaced the bow on her blouse. Beside Miss Field, Fanny felt her own flimsy flowered cotton dress was inadequate cover. She wondered if the secretary disapproved of her. But she gave nothing away. Fanny watched her expression as she looked round the office that had been Mr Burroughs'. Miss Field didn't seem to notice the icon from Ian Ramsey's wall. Just as well, Fanny thought, she'd probably think I stole it.

'Yes, Mrs Dinmont?' Miss Field said.

Fanny tried to look her in the eye, but Miss Field sat staring at the notebook in her lap. Fanny noticed that the steely helmet of hair was quite white on the crown. She felt sorry for the poor woman, getting old must be daunting for someone who was spending all her money to care for elderly relations and might lose the family home that she had counted on inheriting. Fanny tried to imagine what the house in Clapham was like. There'd be pot plants with magenta flowers and she'd put money on antimacassars and a silver-plated teapot with a wooden handle when visitors came, which they probably never did.

Fanny was overwhelmed with pity for the woman. Her voice was particularly gentle as she asked:

'What's the matter, Miss Field?'

Fanny was prepared to hear about the house in Clapham. It was the least she could do. She couldn't imagine Miss Field having many friends she could tell about her worries.

Miss Field raised her head and smiled. She fixed her eyes around Fanny's chin.

'The matter?' she said. 'I don't know what you mean.'

Her tone precluded argument, but Fanny persisted.

'There's something wrong. Is it my fault? I'm not criticizing you, Miss Field, I wouldn't presume. I just want to help.'

Miss Field held on to the defiant smile for a moment. Then her face relaxed into real misery.

'It's Sir Stafford, of course. What else could it be? I'm trying not to be selfish, but suppose he's dead? Suppose he never comes back? What will happen to me?'

Fanny was puzzled. 'But Miss Field,' she said, 'what about the letter? He said he was coming back.'

Miss Field was startled enough to raise her eyes to meet Fanny's.

'A letter?' she said. 'A letter from Sir Stafford? If someone's had a letter, they might have told me.'

'But I thought Ian Ramsey showed you the letter. He said you brought it in to him. I thought he showed it to you.'

'Mr Ramsey did? I don't know what to think. It's all so confusing.'

That, Fanny thought, was true. If Miss Field were really so worried about her future without Sir Stafford, she would surely remember the letter in every detail. But why wouldn't Ian Ramsey show it to her?

Fanny answered her own question. Because the letter wasn't in Sir Stafford's handwriting.

It didn't come from him at all. And if Ian Ramsey said it was Sir Stafford's writing, he was lying. But why should he lie?

Fanny walked round the desk and sat on it beside Miss Field's chair, facing her.

'Look, Miss Field, you've got to tell me the truth. Did you see a letter from Sir Stafford? Any message at all? Did Mr Ramsey say anything to you about it? Try to remember.'

Miss Field stood up. The smile was in place, but her face was flushed.

'No, I don't remember any letter. He probably just forgot. After all, he's a very busy man. He wouldn't realize how much it matters to me . . . on a personal level. So Sir Stafford is taking a few days off, is that right? Thank you for telling me. I'll make the tea.'

She hurried from the room.

Fanny sat down in the chair Miss Field had left. Miss Field's domestic worries were probably distracting her. She must have seen the letter because why would Ian Ramsey write Sir Stafford's letter himself? Did he want to stop further questions? Why? Did he think he could avoid damage to the company? He'd been worried about what the newspapers would make of Sir Stafford's disappearance. Perhaps he'd thought he could stop the situation getting worse. After all, he didn't know that Sir Stafford hadn't killed Mr Burroughs in a car crash and run away. She was the only one, except the guilty party, who knew about that.

Fanny shivered, feeling suddenly frightened. What if Ian Ramsey wrote the letter to try to stop Fanny asking questions? And did he also know that Fanny knew Mr Burroughs hadn't died in a car crash on the Rowfield bypass? And what about Sir Stafford, what had happened to him? If Ian Ramsey faked the letter, he wanted to give the impression that Sir Stafford was all right. Which means, Fanny said to herself, that Sir Stafford is not all right. He could be dead, too.

Fanny's head was spinning. Nothing made sense. Sir Stafford wasn't dead when he was involved in the car crash. He was seen running away by the lorry driver. And what would Ian Ramsey gain by killing Sir Stafford? Nothing that wouldn't come to him soon in the natural course of events, if he wanted sole control of TROD. No, Fanny thought, it doesn't add up. Ian Ramsey isn't a murderer. Either he forgot to mention the letter to Miss Field, or she's so confused and frightened that she didn't take it in.

But Fanny couldn't stop thinking about Sir Stafford. In the end, she called Miss Field on the intercom and asked her to telephone the police station in Oxfordshire who had dealt with Sir Stafford's car crash.

She was put through to Sergeant Kerslake. She recognized his voice. She even thought she heard Inspector Fulwell shouting in the background. She deliberately made her voice sound unlike herself, flat and non-committal.

'I'm ringing from Sir Stafford Williams' office,' she said. 'You may remember he was involved in a car crash with a lorry at the weekend?'

'Yes?' Sergeant Kerslake said.

'I wonder if it's possible to have the lorry driver's home address? We've had a whip-round in the office and wanted to send some flowers and a get well message. Quite unofficial, you understand? Can you help.'

Sergeant Kerslake did not hesitate. 'Quite impossible, madam. That might be prejudicial to any action which may or may not be pending,' he said.

'But there must have been a report of the accident in the local paper. There can't be any secret about it.'

'Of course I can't prevent your using other sources of information,' Sergeant Kerslake said. He put the phone down rather abruptly.

She should have known better than to think the cops would give anything away. She rang Gaylord's number, but no one answered. She would try later, and if he was not at home then, she'd wait and check the lorry driver's address herself in the local paper which would have been delivered to the cottage by the time she got there that night.

She sat down to read a document from a TROD subsidiary somewhere in Africa which apparently existed to support a charitable group dispensing fertiliser. Her mind wandered. The complexities of TROD seemed as remote as the arid plains of Africa where hot gales blew away the life-giving minerals in the soil.

Ian Ramsey came into her office, knocking as he opened the door. He looked ill, paler, his face set like concrete. Startled by his sudden appearance, Fanny jumped to her feet.

'What is it? Is it Sir Stafford?' she cried.

Then she realized that he was furious. He glared at her, his pale eyes like flints.

'What do you think you're doing?' he shouted. 'How dare you meddle in things that don't concern you?'

Fanny sat down again and gave him a cold stare.

'What are you talking about?' she asked.

'You've been ringing the police about Sir Stafford's accident. Don't try and tell me you haven't.'

'If you mean that I asked Miss Field to get me the number of the police down there, it was about something personal. There's no reason you should remember, though I think I told you, but I have a cottage there. The call was in connection with that. But why the hell shouldn't I make inquiries about the crash anyway? I have to deal with press questions. That's what I'm here for.'

He looked at her with contempt.

'Your function is to put off such questions. You don't offer information. The less you know the better.'

'Stop talking such nonsense,' Fanny said. 'I'll do the job I was hired to do and I'll answer to the man who hired me. You had a letter from him saying he'll be back, so until you hear officially that he won't, you are not my boss. If you ever are, I'll leave. Until then, I'd be glad if you would.'

He was taken aback. He hesitated.

'Look,' he said, 'I'm just warning you. There may be charges. You never know. The police may drop it, but perhaps if the other driver thought there was a chance of making some money . . . someone from this office approaching him about the crash could prejudice the course of justice.'

A fair enough point, Fanny thought. Miss Field had evidently listened in to her call and told him what she said. Fanny wished now she had not pretended that the call had nothing to do with Sir Stafford's crash. She supposed she'd panicked, but it was a stupid thing to say.

'Well, perhaps a friendly overture would put the other driver off such action, if he is thinking of taking it,' she said.

'Perhaps it's best left alone.' He smiled, showing his teeth in what she assumed was meant to be a peace-offering. 'There's a lot to be done,' he said.

'True,' Fanny said.

She opened the file on charitable fertilisers and began to read. She heard the door shut behind him as he left. She flicked the switch on the intercom.

'Miss Field, will you bring me the last three year's company reports, please,' she said.

Miss Field cleared her throat and hesitated.

'Miss Field, did you hear me?' Fanny asked.

'Tea with lemon, Miss Dinmont,' Miss Field said. 'Any biscuits?'

She put the phone down before Fanny could reply. Then the door opened and Miss Field came in with a pot of tea and one of the best china cups on a tray.

'Miss Field, what's going on?' Fanny asked. She wondered if the woman had actually gone mad.

Miss Field put down the tray and poured the tea.

'I'm sorry, Miss Dinmont. It's not my fault. I'm not allowed to let anyone see the company reports. Mr Ramsey told me not to, and he was in my room when you asked for them. I thought it better . . .'

'Why? You told him I wanted the police number. Why not tell him this time?'

Miss Field flushed.

'He saw me write down the number from Directory Inquiries. He asked. I can't refuse to tell him when he asks, can I?'

Miss Field was afraid of Ian Ramsey, anyone who bothered to look could see that.

Fanny pressed her.

'Why shouldn't I see the reports? They're published information, aren't they?'

Miss Field shook her head.

'No,' she said, 'I don't think so. It's not a quoted company, it's a family business, you see. And so much of the business is overseas. I know Sir Stafford keeps a lot of the papers at home.'

Miss Field was ill at ease. Fanny handed her a cup of tea.

'You drink this,' she said. 'You seem to need it. Tell me why you seem so frightened. Is it Ian Ramsey'

'I'm not frightened, not really. Its just that if Sir Stafford doesn't come back . . . or decides to retire . . . or even cut back on his workload, I—'

'But your job's safe, surely? Mr Ramsey would keep you on. He'd need your experience.'

'I don't think so, Mrs Dinmont. I don't think Mr Ramsey would have much use for me.'

Fanny didn't know what to say. There was a short silence, then Miss Field took the tray, rattling the cup and saucer as she did so.

The telephone rang as Miss Field left the room. Fanny recognized Ramsey's voice.

'I've got the name and address of that lorry driver you wanted to know,' he said. 'You should have asked me. We had to contact his insurance company. I've had second thoughts.

I think you should go and see him after all. It's a good idea. He might have some light to shed, and you'd find it easier answering questions if you knew his version. Forewarned is forearmed.'

She wrote down what he told her. George Miller, 23 Old Road, Copsey. She knew the place, not far from Rowfield. It had been an American air base during the War, now disused. She remembered driving through it once, when she'd lost her way. An ugly place full of abandoned barracks, with a lot of dilapidated concrete with weeds growing through.

If I lived in a dump like that, Fanny thought, I'd take Sir Stafford Williams for every penny he's got if he drove his car into me. She went to the window and gazed out on the sleek London backwater below, at the coy reproduction gaslights and the wrought-iron window sills and the mellow amber brick glowing in the sunshine. She saw the first signs of autumn colour on the leaves of the plane trees in the far corner of the cul-de-sac, where the cars turned, and pigeons raced for crumbs from the office girls eating sandwiches on the benches outside the elegant railings. A black and white cat washed its face on the steps of the building opposite.

Summer's nearly over, Fanny said to herself. I've sat around doing nothing all summer and now it's nearly over and then it'll be Christmas.

Already the thought depressed her. Last year she'd gone to stay with her mother and step-father in Spain; it was a trying time, she didn't have much skill at bridge. She'd lied to Miss Field when she said she didn't have any family. She always lied about that, well, almost always. Perhaps it was wishful thinking. People told lies all the time, and she wasn't, she supposed, any worse than anyone else. She wondered for a moment if Miss Field could be lying about her ancient mother and aunt. But no, the worry and pain on Miss Field's face was too real. The look on Fanny's face was stubborn. She wasn't going to go to Spain this Christmas, whatever she did. She thought of Gaylord, and wondered if he would spend the holiday in Rowfield. Perhaps he would go back to Connecticut and the former wife and children. Two girls, apparently. He hadn't seen them in two years. Fanny tried to imagine what it would have been like to see her own father every two or three years when she was little.

A taxi outside the TROD office stood with its engine idling. Fanny could see the driver talking over his shoulder to a passenger in the back. The passenger must have mislaid his wallet, for instead of driving away, he got out of the cab and slapped the roof in apology before running up the steps to the front door. Fanny recognized Ian Ramsey. She was surprised that he'd had time to go out and back since he gave her George Miller's address. He must have been on his way out when he rang.

Fanny telephoned Gaylord. The sound of his voice made her feel homesick for Rowfield.

'I was hoping you'd ring,' he said.

'Why? What's wrong?'

'Hold the Cassandra syndrome, will you? Nothing's wrong. It's nice to hear you, and it takes my mind off this bloody blank sheet of paper I've been staring at for three hours.'

'Poor Gaylord!'

'No, on the contrary, lucky Gaylord. Most fortunate Poyntz. We're going to have dinner tomorrow night.'

'We'll be getting ourselves talked about. Having dinner together in public on a Saturday night is as good as a declaration of intent in Rowfield.'

'I have every intention,' Gaylord said. 'What about it?'

Fanny suddenly felt happy. But she had work to do before she could be on the road for Rowfield.

She rang Willie Green, an old pal from her newspaper days.

'I heard you've gone over to the enemy,' he said. 'So what are you trying to sell me? I've always been a sucker for a come on from you.'

Fanny remembered him as a pale and shivering person, always cold-ridden, with too much nose and too little chin. The women journalists nicknamed him Wee Willie.

‘I need you,’ she told Wee Willie.

‘I’m standing to attention,’ he said.

He’d be more at home on the tabloids, Fanny thought, than on that pretentious effort full of social causes and paranoia that he worked for.

She asked him to copy whatever clippings there might be in his newspaper’s library on Sir Stafford Williams.

‘I’ll see what I can do,’ he said. ‘Bad day, you know. We’re frantic here. But for you . . .’

Fanny knew perfectly well that he had not put finger to keyboard all day, perhaps all week.

‘Life and death,’ she said. ‘I’ll buy a bottle of chilled white if you can.’

‘Where there’s a Wee Willie, there’s a way,’ he said.

So he did know what they called him. The joke was on her and the others.

She had scarcely put the phone down when it rang again. This time a reporter from the *Daily Telegraph* wanted to know what Sir Stafford had done in the Second World War.

Fanny asked Miss Field, who looked blank. Several older members of the firm tried to remember.

‘He was connected with the Admiralty,’ said a creaking old man from Personnel.

Fanny reported this back to the *Telegraph* man. She felt like a fool not knowing, it was ridiculous that life at TROD was so secretive.

Unless there were things to hide.

'British Navy?' he asked.

'Did you think it was the German?'

Fanny had found that if you were not sure of your ground, it helped to answer one question with another.

'Suppose not.' The man sounded depressed. 'I'm doing the obit,' he added, 'for the files. Someone here said Sir Stafford did something hush hush in the War but he couldn't remember what.'

'Well,' Fanny said, 'let's both hope it's a long time before it sees the light of print.'

She wasn't meeting Wee Willie in El Vino but in a lesser known bar in Fleet Street. At one time she had spent many evenings there. There weren't any journalists in there nowadays. The only face Fanny recognized was a surprise. Not to have seen Melanie the Animal Rights Maniac for such a long time, and then to see her twice in unexpected places. What *is* her last name? Fanny wondered. Melanie was sitting at a table talking to a woman who had a pen and kept making notes as Melanie talked. The woman with the pen wasn't young. Fanny reckoned she must be a Fleet Street hack nostalgic for the old days who'd made an appointment to meet Melanie in one of her former haunts.

Wee Willie came in, forcing his way through the press of drinkers. Fanny was surprised how pleased she was to see him. I didn't realize how much I've missed it all, she thought.

'What's that woman's name?' she asked him, pointing at Melanie. 'You know her, don't you?'

'You mean Mel Musgrove? Hey, don't tell me life in the sticks has turned you anti? Mind you, I've heard tell you wouldn't mind feeding that smooth bastard you married to the lions in the zoo.'

Fanny laughed. 'That's long over. We're divorced.'

He gave her what she imagined was a comic lustful look.

'You mean my time has come? The cuttings on Sir Stafford were a pretext to call me to your side?'

'Nice of you to offer, but I'm . . . with someone at the moment.'

'I'm glad,' Wee Willie said. 'I hope it works for you. Anyway, you're too late. I'm married . . .'

Melanie Musgrove finished talking to the woman. She stopped to say hello to Fanny as she was leaving.

'I'm living near Rowfield now,' Melanie said, 'across the river in Pyecombe.'

'Taking up huntin', shootin', and fishin'?' Wee Willie asked her. He smiled, but Melanie didn't. The woman with the pen stood behind Melanie looking blank. Fanny saw now that she wasn't a journalist. She had the face of a fanatic. She must be one of Melanie's campaigners against blood sports; or if she wasn't already, she soon would be. Melanie had been converting her, the woman had been taking notes to help in her own conversion. Now that Melanie was living across the river from Rowfield Fanny wondered if she still had a copy of *Memoirs of a Foxhunting Man* in her bookcase. She'd have to get it out on the coffee table in case Melanie came to call.

Melanie and her new recruit left and Willie went to the bar to get more drinks. Fanny glanced through the photocopies he had brought about Sir Stafford.

The clippings told Fanny very little. The company was run through a trust registered in Liechtenstein. There was mention of small acquisitions, the odd charitable gift, a social occasion. Someone had attempted a profile of Sir Stafford. He was quoted saying that he liked to buy overseas companies as a way of breaking down the barriers between peoples. 'Buying and selling is communication,' he'd said. 'It transcends language and cultural difference.'

The interviewer had asked whether one man should have so much power through being rich. 'Money itself isn't a source of power,' Sir Stafford had told him, 'power comes from what you make money do.'

'Any good?' Willie asked, coming back from the bar and puffing and blowing as if it had been a hard journey. Then he started telling her about his wife and the new baby and the kitchen units he was putting in himself.

By the time she got away from London it was much later than she'd intended. As she drove into The Black Bull car park, the last drinkers were lurching out of the bar.

She decided this time to walk round to the front door of the cottage. The lane was dark and full of shadows. There was a lamp in a bedroom window of one of the cottages, and she could hear a baby crying. She opened her front door carefully, trying not to make any noise, and leaned in to turn on the lobby light.

The place was exactly as she'd left it. What she'd expected she wasn't certain, but the weakness of her knees when she sat down on the settee by the sliding glass door, with the central heating boiler humming and a mug of coffee clutched in her hands, told her she had been putting off the moment of returning here. Now she was glad to be home with no surprises on the sitting-room floor.

CHAPTER FOURTEEN

Gaylord arrived at the cottage at lunchtime the next day. They went to The Bull, but Gaylord wouldn't eat. 'Let me lubricate my ears first, will you, no one can listen on a dry throat.'

Fanny pulled him into a corner and in a low voice told him about Ian Ramsey, the letter from Sir Stafford, and about the way Miss Field seemed to be cracking up.

'They're in it together,' Gaylord said, 'no doubt about it. Villains, every one. Straight out of central casting. What's the matter with you? Miss Marple would have been on to them right away, and she'd have kept knitting and never dropped a stitch.'

Then she told him about Percy Parfitt and Piers Scruton.

'Do you know Scruton?' she asked.

'He's here now.' He turned and shouted across the bar, 'Hey, Piers, come over here and have a word with this young woman, will you.'

Fanny knew by sight the man who broke away from a group laughing and drinking champagne on the far side of the room. He spent a lot of time here in the bar, but he was different from the other regulars. He was always at the centre of a party of youngish men and women who looked as though they had stepped out of advertisements in an upmarket country lifestyle magazine.

'What ho, old horse,' he now said to Gaylord in a comic tone of voice. 'How's the funny business?'

'Ms Dinmont wants to meet you,' Gaylord said.

'Will you have a drink?' she asked. She was appalled. Surely this man could never be a world authority on icons.

He shook his head. 'Thanks, but no. I'll have to get back to my party pronto.' He turned to Gaylord, held up crossed fingers, and said in a conspiratorial whisper, 'The man in the cravat with the artfully rumpled blonde is furnishing a country house outside Abingdon. They're interested in instant ancestral *objets*, and I think I've got them hooked.'

'They're all men in cravats with artfully rumpled blondes,' Gaylord said. 'How do you tell them apart?'

Piers shrugged. 'Who cares, as long as someone buys? Now what can I do for you?'

'Oh, my friend here is thinking of doing a bit of speculation. What's the form on Coptic iconography?'

'You're kidding me!' Piers said. He seemed unsure whether to laugh. But then he suddenly became a different person. He cast away his jovial bluster.

'Hey,' Gaylord said to Fanny, 'look at the hawk seeing prey!'

'Someone I know was talking about Crusader icons,' Fanny said, but Gaylord kicked her under the table. When she looked at him to protest, he shook his head at her in warning. Good God, she thought, he even suspects Piers. And then she remembered the break in at Bentham's, and she saw the point of being cautious.

'They sounded interesting and rare,' she said to Piers. 'Gaylord thought you might know something about them.' It sounded lame.

'Alas, old love, I wish I did. There's very little to know, so far. There's never been enough to go on, just the Sinai collection they found at St Catherine's monastery. Even less than the works from Wallachia and Moldavia, which *are* opening up to us now. In terms of their post-Byzantine icons, that is. The Coptics are more or less a closed book so far, I'm afraid.' He frowned, then added, 'I suppose all that may be due for a change.' He sounded doubtful.

'What do you mean, a change?' Fanny asked.

Piers seemed puzzled. 'Well,' he said, 'they'll be coming out as the political situation gets worse.'

'Sorry, I'm not with you? What do you mean, coming out?'

'Oh, it often happens with art treasures. Political instability means the threatened people or groups in a country try to flog their art treasures to get out. Or they flee and bring them with them to sell when they get out. It's always been a recognized trade. Or the governments sell them, like Cromwell and the Puritans did. The James the Fourth Book of Hours is in Vienna now, for example. The Puritans even sold the twelfth century Psalter of Couper Angus Abbey to the Vatican. They didn't let principles stand in the way of business. Things haven't changed. And actually it's an ill wind and all that. We'll be glad enough to get our hands on the Coptic stuff when it starts coming out of Ethiopia, for instance. If we can afford it.'

'Ah, there's the rub,' Gaylord said.

Piers looked thoughtful.

'There does seem to be something afoot, now you mention it,' he said. 'It's the bane of my life, actually. People look on these things as an investment and a hedge against the inevitably disastrous future. When the time comes, they'll do exactly what the poor Ethiopians and their kind are doing. Pre-convertible currency, damn their eyes.'

'About something afoot?' Fanny prompted him.

'Oh, yes. Funny you should mention Crusader icons, that's all. I had some fellow coming down to see me about one the other day. Wanted me to tell him what it was worth. I asked how he'd come by it, but he was vague. I thought I'd better look at it and then ask questions.'

Fanny and Gaylord exchanged glances.

'What was his name?' Fanny asked, and then she wished she hadn't because the expression on Piers' face clearly pleaded the Fifth Amendment on client confidentiality. 'What happened?' she added quickly.

She tried to keep the excitement out of her

voice.

'Fellow never came. He dragged me out to the shop from home in the middle of the night because he said he couldn't get here earlier, and then never turned up. It was a bad night, actually. First I got a call that somebody was asking for me here at The Bull so I thought it must be this party and went rushing out to find there was no one there at all and they didn't know anything about it. Weren't any too pleased to be knocked up, either. Then when I'd gone back and locked up the shop, had a few drinks and gone home to bed the police were on the phone about the burglary.'

'Perhaps he missed you while you were here at The Bull?' Fanny said.

'No, he can't have come at all.' Piers looked embarrassed. 'I left the door to the office open so he could go in, but no one had been there. I was only a few minutes. Oh, it happens all the time. He probably got cold feet. Thinks I'll find out he didn't pay the import duty, I expect.' He laughed.

'What was his name?' Gaylord asked. 'The man with the icon?'

Piers shifted on his seat.

'Well, that's just it,' he said. 'I don't know. He didn't say, and I didn't want to ask too many questions and put him off.'

'But surely—?' Fanny interrupted.

'It sounds silly, I know. But most of the stuff I sell is spoiled for me by the time I get my hands on it. It's changed hands too often, for money. Now a Crusader icon—it would be like a virgin to Bluebeard for me. It might be here because some greedy little despot is selling off the national heritage to save his skin, or to get treasure hunters in the West to finance his horrid little coup in return, but for centuries it's been pure, no idea of money value or greed—' Piers broke off. 'Sorry,' he said. 'Getting rather carried away. Don't take any notice. Who am I to talk? People can dress it up as they like, though, but there are really very few things you can do with money when you come down to it.'

Gaylord nodded.

'I sometimes think that's what drives the rich to get richer,' he said. 'They can't believe that's all there is to it. Even so, just give me the chance to test the theory!'

Piers went back to his party. They heard his loud laughter as they got up to go.

'Well, where does that lead us, my dear Watson?' Gaylord asked as they walked up the street in the dusty sunshine. 'Has Holmes a theory?' Fanny said.

'Early days, early days,' Gaylord said. 'But no.'

'By the way,' Fanny said, trying to sound casual, 'what does this Harry Hughes of yours do for his millions?'

Gaylord considered this. 'You know, that's a mystery. For all I know he could steal

Crusader icons.'

'But seriously.'

'Seriously, I don't really know. Maybe he told me once, but I can't remember.'

She brought up the subject again over dinner and then once more in bed, but he still couldn't remember, and then romance got in the way of her curiosity.

She was happy. Gaylord Poyntz had driven the ghost of Alan out of the big brass bed. But his ghost hadn't left the cottage entirely. Fanny had the feeling he might be standing in the corner watching; and, of course, there was the ghost of poor Mr Burroughs stretched out downstairs on the sitting-room floor.

CHAPTER FIFTEEN

On Sunday evening Fanny zipped her weekend bag and said to Gaylord, 'I'll go out the back. Will you lock the glass door and slam the Yale as you go out the front?'

'Oh,' he said, 'didn't I tell you? I'm coming with you.'

'No, you didn't tell me,' she said.

'Yeah. The dogs can stay with my neighbour. I've got something in mind, as a matter of fact.'

Fanny thought he meant that he had designs on her. 'Oh, really?' she said. She was pleased, but she didn't want him to know it.

But Gaylord explained his plan to her in her car as she negotiated the heavy traffic of weekenders returning to London. 'I'm going to do a bit of sketching,' he said.

'Sketching?'

'Yeah, I thought I would. A whole series of "Glimpses of Picturesque Olde England" come to mind. Starting with a picturesque corner of the ancient City.'

'A charming leisure pursuit,' she said. It was none of her business if he didn't share her preoccupation with solving Mr Burroughs' murder.

'You don't understand,' he said. 'What I do is, I set myself up outside your office and get drawing. You'll find that Sherlock Holmes often put on a disguise like that. No one will think twice about an elderly tourist sketching a historic London backwater. This whole business involves TROD, or at least people who work there. I'll make quick sketches of the people who go in and out of your offices, and then we can take the pictures round Rowfield and see if anyone recognizes anyone. You see?'

Fanny didn't see but she thought it best not to say so. She was touched that he wanted to help. She felt that there was something shocking about the way people had taken poor Mr Burroughs' death for granted. It didn't seem to make much difference to them whether he was alive or dead.

Gaylord seemed to echo her unspoken thoughts. 'Someone must know something,' he said.

Yes, she thought, walking up the cul-de-sac to the TROD building the next morning, someone must know something. But people might not know that what they knew was important.

It seemed hopeless, though, and it depressed her. She kicked a Coca Cola can which the dustmen had missed on their rounds earlier. Already, first thing in the morning, there was a faint fast-food smell of fat and onions wafting across from a sandwich bar nearby. Life was going on.

At the top of the stairs on her way to her own room Fanny passed Miss Field. The bow was back at the neck of the shapeless suit. Does Miss Field think anyone cares whether she lives or dies? Fanny asked herself. Of course the mother and aunt in Clapham do, but apart from them, if Miss Field was suddenly found dead on the floor they'd clear her up and life would go on with all memory of her quickly fading. Something had to be done to stop that happening to Mr Burroughs.

Fanny slammed the door of her room behind her. She wanted to cry. She put her handbag on the desk and walked across to the window. She leaned her cheek against the cool glass. A motor cycle messenger revved his harsh engine outside. She watched him skitter through parked cars out of the cul-de-sac on to the busy twenty-first century street beyond. There was no sign of Gaylord.

She'd given him a spare set of keys to the flat and left him in bed. Several times during the morning she checked the window to see if he had taken up his role as street artist. She thought perhaps he had given up the idea, but towards noon she looked again and saw him stride across the street towards the TROD office. She thought at first he was wearing trainers, but then she saw they were old-fashioned white buckskin shoes.

She watched him spend much time turning and testing views with angles made with his hands in a way she could not believe anyone who saw him could think natural. There was something else, too, which made him look wrong. Fanny did not spot it at first. He was the only person in the street on this glorious late-summer Monday morning who actually looked happy.

Fanny saw a group of girls pass by and stop, peering over his shoulder to see what he was doing. One of them pretended to pose like a pin-up girl. Gaylord's pencil flowed. Then he tore off the page and gave it to her.

There was a knock on the door. Fanny turned away from the window. Ian Ramsey had come into the room. He walked over and stood beside her, staring down at Gaylord.

'Oh, another of those artist fellows. The good weather brings them out. They're usually dreadful, you know, can't get the basics right. They always manage to make this building look like Mummy and Daddy's house by Fred, age six.' Ramsey smiled but the smile showed no sentiment about Fred, age six. 'I think the sketching is a cover for picking up girls,' he added.

'Oh, well, as long as it makes someone happy,' she said, moving back to her desk. 'Did you want something?'

'Oh, yes,' he said, flicking his forehead with his finger. 'I've been thinking. You really should go down and see that lorry driver fellow. It would be worth finding out what his attitude is, in case the press get to him. We haven't heard from Sir Stafford since that first rather cryptic message. It's becoming a bit of a mystery, don't you think?'

'Yes, I do. I told you last week, I intended to speak to him. But Mr Miller isn't on the phone. I suppose I could go and see if I can track him down next weekend while I'm in Rowfield. Copsey's only a few miles away.

'No time like the present,' Ian Ramsey said. 'Why don't you get down there today.' He sounded cheerful. 'Take a taxi.'

'Oh, I'll drive.'

'No you won't. It's all on the firm's account. It'll give you a chance to make notes on the way back.'

'It seems silly to go back there when I've only just come up.'

'It'll give you a day off.' He gave her his good-looking smile.

Fanny gave in. George Miller, if he was at home, might be able to shed some light on the mystery of the car crash and Sir Stafford's disappearance. And if he wasn't at home she could always think of something that needed doing at the cottage before coming back to London.

'I might as well go now,' she said. 'There's nothing on.' She picked up the intercom to ask Miss Field to call a cab on the TROD account.

'It's all done,' Ramsey said. 'I told Miss Field I was going to suggest you went today, and she said she'd take care of the cab. I think she hopes you may turn up something to explain Sir Stafford's absence. She's lost without him, you know.'

Fanny wanted to make some slight protest that he was rail-roading her. But when he mentioned Miss Field's feelings she felt it would be churlish to object.

'You should enjoy the drive,' he said.

He seemed determined to be friendly. Fanny watched him as he leaned against the window sill. What's he after? she wondered. She had reason to want to find out if Miller could shed any light on Mr Burroughs' murder, but what was Ian Ramsey's game? He wants me out of the office, she thought. Why?

'It's here already,' he said. 'Your taxi awaits.'

Fanny called out to Miss Field as she went out. 'I'll be in tomorrow if I don't get back today.'

'Very well, Mrs Dinmont,' Miss Field said from her room and there seemed no life in her voice at all. Fanny's depression had lifted, but she could tell how Miss Field was feeling. She stopped and went back, looking round the door to where Sir Stafford's secretary sat at her desk.

'Cheer up, Miss Field,' Fanny said. 'It may be good news.'

Miss Field looked down and stabbed at a pad of paper on the desk with a ballpoint pen. 'Yes, Mrs Dinmont,' she said.

Fanny ran down the stairs and out into the street. The taxi's engine was running. Damn, she thought, I can't tell Gaylord what's happening. She walked round and opened the cab door on the driver's side, loudly telling the driver over her shoulder to go to Copsey. She wanted Gaylord to hear her. He should know that she would be late home.

'The secretary gave me the address,' the driver said. He reached out of his cab window to shut the passenger door where it had not fully locked as she got in.

'Your meter's not working,' she said. 'Don't you charge waiting?'

'Account and out of town. No meters,' he said.

He drove off with a jerk. What a thug, Fanny thought. She saw Gaylord still seated on his stool under a plane tree. He was staring at the front of the TROD building with a ruminative look on his face, apparently oblivious to anything going on in the street. He gave no sign of seeing her.

The taxi swung out into the heavy traffic outside the cul-de-sac. Just my luck, she thought, I would get landed with a cowboy. As the driver jumped the lights on Moorgate, she tried to slide back the communicating window to tell him to slow down. It was stuck. Obviously he's jammed it to stop complaints at his driving, Fanny thought. But at least he wouldn't be able to carry on a conversation. She sat back, taking an impotent dislike to his burly neck and his cropped dark hair. She hated him, too, for the four 'Thank You For Not Smoking' signs in the back of the cab and the thump of the bass line of rock music on his radio. She could see him swilling lager outside Millwall football ground on a Saturday. I'll bet he's got tattoos on his bum, she thought.

Through the window she watched suburban gardens give way to paddocks and fields. Ian Ramsey's right, she thought, it's a beautiful day for a drive.

They came round a sharp corner into the village street of Old Copsey. The driver slowed to manoeuvre between parked cars, then accelerated again as they moved away from the pretty stone cottages and walled gardens gathered round a church and out into flat, deserted countryside. Soon Fanny could see Copsey itself, a dilapidated jumble of huts on the old airfield, and the ranks of abandoned prefabricated houses around it. Even the sunlight which had polished the original old village cast no cheer on the dun-faced dwellings stained and muddied by damp, bedraggled among overgrown grass and rampant brambles.

The driver slowed, peering out of his cab as they moved along row upon row of these houses. The dreary and defaced homes gave way to even poorer buildings, hung with asbestos sheeting and corrugated iron. Those without boarded windows had broken glass panes. Sometimes a greyish tatter of net slapped idly against the window frame in the slight wind. Ahead Fanny could see the high link chain fence surrounding the old airbase itself, with the concrete runway stretching ahead, crazed with grassy cracks, towards the unused hangars and abandoned huts.

The taxi stopped at the end of a sordid little row of houses. The driver leaned out of his window and opened the passenger door for her.

'Are you sure?' she asked, unwilling to get out.

'Don't look much, does it? But it's the place all right.'

He pointed to a number on a broken gate.

Fanny looked back the way they'd come. Nothing moved.

'It looks as if there's been a nuclear war,' she said.

'Well, this is the address given,' the driver said. 'Miller, 23 Old Road, Copsey. Looks like it's been a bleedin' squat, don't it?'

Fanny got out of the taxi. She hesitated. I'm being feeble, she told herself. All I have to do is make sure there's no one here.

She took a deep breath, knowing the taxi driver was watching her. What harm could come to her with this burly London cabby sitting so comfortingly churlish in his taxi at the garden gate just dying to put the boot or the head in on someone?

She walked up the overgrown path to the front door. There were signs of life. Someone had used the path recently; she could see where recent footsteps had crushed the weeds. Fanny pushed back seeding nettles with her shoulder bag held in front of her like a shield. Underfoot the old paving stones were treacherous with slime.

Once at the front door she looked back at the taxi. The driver had taken out a copy of the *Sun* newspaper and propped it against the wheel to read it. Fanny felt reassured. She knocked at the door. There was no answer, but the door wasn't locked or even closed properly; it swung slowly open.

There was no obvious sign of life.

'Anyone there?' Fanny called. Her voice echoed in the small stairwell, sounding wooden, like a bad actress's.

There was someone in the house, she was sure of it. She could feel it. Or if there wasn't now, there had been very recently.

'Mr Miller?' she called, moving slowly and carefully into the hall.

There was some small sound she could not identify. She could not even be certain she had really heard anything. Mice, perhaps, even rats. The sound came again. Fanny took a deep breath and opened a door off the hall which might lead to a living-room.

It was dark inside. She moved further into the room. She had made a mistake. It was not a living room. There was no window, only a narrow skylight high up on the far wall. She stretched out her left arm and felt the warm touch of spiders' webs thick against a damp wall. It's a lavatory, she said to herself. She could see the loo and a cistern high up on the wall. It was a peculiar room with the high ceiling and skylight. She supposed it had been put in by the Americans during the War.

She started to back out into the hall, but the door banged shut behind her. She jumped. The noise startled her and she was in the dark now.

She swung round and came up against the closed door. She scrabbled to find the edge, feeling her way down, looking for a knob or handle. There was none. All she could feel was the outside edge of a keyhole.

CHAPTER SIXTEEN

'You stupid cow,' Fanny said to herself aloud. 'Now look what you've gone and done. Either you've locked yourself in or you've walked into a trap.' And either way, you're well and truly buggered, she added silently.

She squatted on her heels to peer through the keyhole. She could see nothing.

She began to shout. The Millwall supporter taxi driver might hear her between the thunderous bouts of music on his radio. Keep your head, she said to herself, he'll come looking for you. He'll notice you've been gone a long time and come looking.

Fumbling in her shoulder bag she felt for the smooth outline of her Swiss Army penknife. She carried this as a slight affectation, but nevertheless found it useful for cleaning her nails and opening impregnable packages.

With the open blade she explored the inside of the keyhole. There was a key in there all right. An unusually big key.

She felt her way carefully down the door frame, using her fingers to follow the edge.

She lay down and tried to peer under the door at floor level. If there was room, she could prod the key out of the lock and slide it back underneath the door. She poked the crevice with the knife, and felt thick dust fill her mouth. That'll teach me to have my mouth hanging open when I concentrate, she thought. Then she started sneezing.

The sound seemed shatteringly loud. A silence deeper than before followed. A deliberate silence. Fanny suddenly realized that there was someone outside the door.

It occurred to her all of a sudden that it might be the Millwall supporter who had locked her in. But why? Unless he was a rapist playing some moronic game. Fanny shivered. Miller's house was as cold as a tomb and she was wearing a thin cotton dress. She'd left her linen jacket in the taxi.

She shouted again. 'Help! Mr Miller? Help me!'

She leaned against the door, her ear to the panel.

'Come on, for gawd's sake,' a man muttered. So there were more than one of them out there.

The same man spoke again, in answer to a question, apparently. 'Who'll hear her? There's no one for miles around. We've got to get the stuff loaded.'

Fanny felt close to panic. What had happened? Was George Miller of 23 Old

Road, Copsey, some kind of pervert? Or was he a criminal and she'd interrupted a robbery of some sort. Did Mr Miller in fact exist? I've only got Ian Ramsey's word for it, Fanny thought. He's the one who sent me here. In which case, Ramsey had set her up, and the Millwall supporter could be the other man. But Ian Ramsey didn't want me to come here at first, Fanny thought. Did he suspect that Miller and the car crash were a set-up? In which case it could be the absent Sir Stafford who had masterminded whatever it was that was going on.

Fanny heard floorboards creak and a door slam, then the unmistakable engine-note of a London taxi. The noises seemed muffled. The walls must be thicker than they looked. She fumbled her way to the lavatory and sat down. I must think, she said to herself, but thinking only makes me realize how frightened I am.

She stretched out her arms to either side. She could not even straighten them. Her cage was about four feet across. When she measured fore and aft in the same way, from behind the lavatory to the door was just beyond her reach, perhaps six or seven feet. Fanny felt a momentary fussy indignation that councils were so mean when they planned their cramped municipal homes. Or was the military responsible in this case? It was a curious design, in either case, with the skylight marking the top of the wall a long way above her reach.

The skylight was her only hope of escape. It was above the cistern. The glass was so dirty that it provided little light, but it was the only way to the outside.

Fanny took off her shoes and put them in the shoulder bag. She then slung the bag across her chest. She turned sideways on the lavatory seat and raised her legs to push against the wall with her feet, then she pressed her back against the wall. This was something she had heard mountain climbers did. They apparently climbed like this up narrow passages between rocks. Kids also sometimes did it in door jambs. Thank God for long legs, she thought, anyone short wouldn't have a prayer. But it was hard work.

Several times she had to start again. Her stockinged feet slipped on the damp wall and she had to come down and take her stockings off. Then her skirt kept getting in the way. She scooped up the thin cotton and wound it into a knot and tucked it into its own waistband.

The first steps each time were quite easy, but gradually the unused muscles in her thighs and calves protested. Her legs trembled, and the pain in her lower back where she inched herself upwards against the wall grew urgent. She spent longer and longer resting between each upward movement, but she could not ease the muscles without losing her hold.

Once she made a false move and only just

dropped her legs in time to break her fall across the lavatory seat. She sat there for a while, her head on her knees to try to ease her muscles.

It's no good, she thought, I can't do it. It's impossible.

But there was nothing else for it. She knew there was little chance of anyone rescuing her. No one knew where she'd gone except Ian Ramsey, but it seemed to be his henchmen who had put her here. Miss Field did, but Miss Field wouldn't wonder where she was until tomorrow, and then she'd ask Ramsey, and he'd say he'd sent her out on another job for a few days. Gaylord? Fanny imagined Gaylord searching for her. He'd start asking questions at a pub and he wouldn't get much further.

She gritted her teeth and started to inch her way upwards once again.

Above her head the filthy rectangle of glass grew darker as daylight faded. She was level with the cistern. It blocked her way. Very carefully, her legs quivering, she shuffled sideways until she could feel it under her thighs. From here she could lever herself up to reach the sill of the skylight.

The skylight was not designed to open. She pressed against the walls as hard as she could with her back and left leg to keep herself in place while she swung her right foot to kick the frame. Three times she kicked but the skylight didn't give, and each time she kicked she was seized with a fear of falling and breaking her back. She realized she could not break the glass that way.

Balancing herself with head and left shoulder against the wall, she pushed her right hand into the shoulder bag. She could feel herself slipping but she found the Swiss Army knife. She drew it out and, leaning back so that her spine took most of her weight, she raised the knife to her mouth and used her teeth to lever the blade open. Then, pressing with all her might to keep from falling, she leaned forward and began to work the knife into the join between wood and glass.

The frame was rotten, but the glass, she discovered, was reinforced with wire. She managed to loosen a strand, then a link. Sliding the knife handle through this to give her purchase, she jerked as hard as she could.

The wire peeled away from the rotten wood. The glass dropped away. The skylight was open.

There was little room to manoeuvre between the sill and the ceiling. She had to inch back into the flying buttress position between the two walls before, pressing as hard as she could with one leg and arm, she was able to turn herself over and slide through the skylight backwards, feet first, her hands clutching at the rotten frame. There was a drop of twenty feet or more to the ground.

I'll break my neck, she thought.

She began to slip down, scrabbling with her feet against the rendered concrete of the outside wall.

She dropped into a spiky horticultural Manhattan of stalks. Her bag, dragged after her by the strap, hit her on the head. Her legs were scratched and bleeding. She got to her feet, feeling her way around the wall to a patch of clearer ground.

Here her first instinct was to put on her shoes and start running.

It was growing dark, but not as dark as it had been inside. Fanny, leaning against the wall to fasten her shoes, heard voices round at the front of the house. There were people who lived in this desolate street. She was preparing herself to go to them and ask for help when she heard one of them say, 'She can't get away.'

Another said, 'What about the geezer?'

With a sinking heart Fanny recognized the voice of the Millwall supporter.

'He's tied up,' the first man said. 'He'll never get out. We've time for a pint.'

So she had not been the only prisoner in the house. Feeling her way along the wall, she made out another door at ground level. She wanted to run, but if there was someone else locked up in the house, she couldn't leave. She was shaking with fear but she must at least try to see if she could help the other prisoner.

She tried to open the door, but it was

locked. Then she saw that the key was in the lock. That's odd, she thought. People usually want to keep intruders out, not in, when they locked outside doors.

She turned the key and tried the door again. The lock was free but the door stuck. She peered closer. It was bolted, top and bottom.

I really should run, she thought, go to Inspector Fulwell, breathe in his face so he knows I haven't been drinking and then tell him the story.

She slid back the bolts and the door opened easily. It had obviously been oiled recently. Fanny glanced behind her round the garden. There was no sound at all. Nature was evidently holding its breath too. She moved cautiously forward into the house. This is crazy, she thought.

It was a kitchen. There was a tap dripping somewhere in the dark. Fanny could make out cracks of gloomy light through a boarded window. She pushed back the door behind her, to let in as much light as possible. Then she stepped into the room.

She tripped over something soft on the floor and jumped back. She bent to feel what it was. It was a blanket, damp to the touch.

Then a hand suddenly grasped her, catching her hair. She gasped in terror, pulling away as if she had touched a snake.

'Who are you?' a small voice whispered close to her face.

She jumped again.

'Who is it?' she said. She was trembling. Her hand closed on her knife in her shoulder bag and she pulled it out. Very carefully she moved forward, the blade outstretched in front of her.

With her left hand, she felt rough dry skin. A man's voice, hoarse and weak, rasped, 'I heard them shut someone else in. Is that you?'

'Yes, I suppose it is.' Fanny's voice sounded higher than she'd expected. 'Unless this house is full of people like us.'

'I know you,' the man said. He was not only hoarse and weak, he was old. 'I know your voice. It's Mrs Dinmont, isn't it? They planned it all, you know, I heard them. Days ago, talking about you. They said you were asking questions.'

'Sir Stafford? Is that you?' Fanny ran her hand across a bony face, thin, stiff hair, bony shoulders.

'I must have been here for days. Weeks, I don't know. I'm tied up, you see. Can you let me loose?'

Fanny got to work with her knife.

'You didn't mention this in the job specification,' she said.

She put the knife back in her bag and grasped Sir Stafford by the arm. He winced as she gripped him, and she loosened her hold.

'We'd better get the hell out of here. Can you move?' she asked. She could hear that she sounded as though she was bullying him.

'It's all very well for a young thing like you,' he said. 'I'm an old man.'

'Have they been feeding you?' she asked.

'Oh, yes,' Sir Stafford said. 'They want to keep me alive for some reason.' He made a sound that could have been a wry laugh. 'I wish I knew their game,' he added.

Sir Stafford made an effort to get to his feet. 'We've got to get away from here,' he said. 'They'll be back.'

She grabbed one of his thin arms and put it round her neck, then she lifted him.

'No, no,' he said, 'you go. Leave me here and you go and get help.'

'There's no help near enough. And they might discover I'm missing and by the time I've convinced the police that I'm telling the truth and get back here with them they'll have moved you.' She could see Inspector Fulwell's face if she started trying to explain to him. 'Our only chance is for them not to find us. Come on.'

She hauled him out of the door and through the undergrowth. It was getting darker, which was good for cover, but made it difficult to see where they were going. They tottered through bushes, across a half-rotted vegetable patch and through a broken fence into another neglected and abandoned back garden beyond.

'Do you know where we're going?' Sir Stafford asked. He was already short of breath.

They skirted two other deserted and half-derelict houses. Then, breaking through a skimpy hedge, they were on a pavement.

Sir Stafford leaned heavily on her. 'Well, which way?' she said. 'We've got to try to find the main road.' A road with people, she thought, and cars.

They moved off slowly, entwined like lovers in the shadows.

'Who are they?' Fanny asked. 'Who's behind this?'

'There's someone in my company involved in it, whatever it is,' Sir Stafford said. Fanny could hear the distress in his voice. 'There's the driver, the one who brought you here, he's one. There's one that came round twice. A different type, well-spoken, but I didn't recognize the voice. Then there's another called Miller. I heard the driver call him George. None of them masterminds.'

'Let's hope not,' Fanny said. 'We must get out of these bloody little streets on to a proper road soon.' She had to keep up Sir Stafford's spirits. He was a man of power, but he wasn't used to the outside world. He was a man who usually didn't even get rained on.

She felt unsafe as they staggered off down the road although the dark street was deserted. There was a small copse, a patch of scrub and undergrowth and she made for that. There they could crawl off the road and sit down to give Sir Stafford a rest. Herself, too, as she was out of breath at the effort of half-carrying him.

But they had scarcely collapsed behind a tangle of overgrown hazel branches and dense blackthorn scrub when she realized she had made a mistake.

'It's them,' Sir Stafford whispered.

He was right. Fanny caught a glimpse of the Millwall supporter looming through a barrier of thorn and twigs. He was making a tremendous din trampling through the undergrowth. He wasn't used to being off the beaten track, and the man with him was no better. They kept swearing as they were slapped by rebounding thorn-covered branches, but they were heading in the right direction, straight for where Fanny and Sir Stafford lay flat on a bed of some sour-smelling weed. And Fanny knew they weren't very well hidden. In the half-light of the moon she could see the two men's faces quite clearly. Any moment now they were going to step on her legs and see her thighs gleaming white in the moonlight through her ripped skirt. She held the Swiss army knife ready.

'Fuck this,' the Millwall supporter said. 'They won't be in this jungle. They'll be legging it down the road looking for a copper.'

'You're right,' the other man said.

Fanny saw them turn back the way they had come, stumbling as they crashed away through the undergrowth. They would get the Millwall supporter's taxi and start looking through the derelict streets.

'We don't have much time,' she said to Sir Stafford, and she pulled him up and helped him through the dense thicket of blackthorn towards the road.

There she tried to make him move faster, pressing him to hurry, but he was feeble and weak.

She did not hear the car approach, coming slowly round the corner. Suddenly they were trapped in the arc of headlights, like rabbits on a night road unable to move.

CHAPTER SEVENTEEN

Fanny's teeth began to chatter. Sir Stafford went limp, hanging on her shoulder like a doll. The car stopped. Blinded in the car lights, she heard a door open, then the sound of someone walking calmly towards them. She could feel herself trembling. Up to the point when the door banged behind her in that broken-down house, she'd been playing a game. Even the body on the floor hadn't seemed real, the whole thing like an elaborate charade lightened by the romance with Gaylord. But now she was shaking with real fear.

'Sir Stafford Williams, I presume?' a voice in the dark said. 'Gaylord?' Fanny whispered.

'Who else would it be?'

'For God's sake, Gaylord! We're being pursued by a gang of homicidal crooks.'

'Say, are you really? Like in the movies? If so, we'd better get the hell out of here.'

He took Sir Stafford and bundled him into the back seat of the car.

'This is my car,' Fanny said. 'What are you doing with my car?'

'I thought you said you're being pursued by a gang of murderers. I'm just a car thief. Get in.'

'I'll drive,' Fanny said.

Fanny put the car in gear and let in the clutch. The engine stalled. Her hands were still shaking, and her legs too.

'Sorry,' Fanny said, restarting. 'Now which way?'

'Right,' Gaylord said.

She saw the battered cul-de-sac sign just in time, and swerved to the left.

'I meant left,' Gaylord said. 'When I said right, I meant left.'

'My God,' Sir Stafford said from the backseat.

'I think you should take the next right,' Gaylord said.

'D'you mean left?'

'That way,' he said, waving a hand in the dark.

The road swung round, and Fanny pulled the wheel over as hard as she could. The tyres screeched as they slewed across the road. The headlamps picked out the shape of a London taxicab parked facing them. Fanny could see the startled face of the Millwall supporter at the wheel. There was no sign of the second man.

Fanny accelerated. The taxi's headlights appeared behind her as the driver turned to follow.

On the straight she was faster than the taxi, but she lost time with hesitation over which way to go. One faceless line of deserted houses followed another. She had an idea she might be going round in a circle.

Then, quite suddenly, she reached a T-junction. A car, full headlamps glaring, flashed from the right with a howling of horn. It was the main road. She was twenty yards ahead of her pursuer. She turned left. She knew where she was now. She made for Rowfield.

The taxi was still behind them. Sometimes as they turned a corner at a twist in the road the lights disappeared from the rear view mirror, but they always returned.

'He's still there,' she said to Gaylord.

'Yes,' he said, 'he's still there.' He sounded like a tourist being shown an ancient monument.

'Well,' she said, 'fancy meeting you in a place like this.'

'A truly civilized person is at home in all surroundings,' Gaylord said.

'Gaylord, what were you doing there? How did you get there?'

'Well, there I was, just sitting in that street all doubled up on a doll's house stool with my knees giving me hell— Can you imagine what it's like for a man with legs as long as mine crouching like that for hours on end? Then this cab drives up and the driver sits there chatting on one of those mobile phones. Then out you come and say "Take me to Copsey" in the ringing tones of a long tradition of hockey fields—'

'Lacrosse, actually,' Fanny said.

'—and he drives off with you. Incidentally, he's still behind us.'

'I know he's still there.'

'Just so long as my fascinating story doesn't let you forget it,' Gaylord said cheerfully.

'Well, what happened then? What made you follow?'

'I was coming to that. I wish you wouldn't interrupt all the time. I can't think you were ever much of a journalist. You never listen.'

'For Heaven's sake, man, get on with it,' Sir Stafford said from the back seat.

'You all right there?' Gaylord asked, twisting round to peer at Sir Stafford.

'Gaylord!' Fanny cried.

'Well, if you're sitting comfortably, I'll continue. I thought it was a bit queer when this cab drove away because all those black cabs have numbers on the back, and this one didn't.

Now that struck me as unusual.'

'Perhaps he didn't need one. Ian Ramsey said he was on account, perhaps he's employed by the firm.'

'No, he isn't,' Sir Stafford said. 'We have an account with a taxi firm, we don't own it. As a matter of fact I thought of buying a black taxi once, when there was a kidnapping scare. Thought you couldn't be much safer and more anonymous than in a London taxi.'

Gaylord said, 'Can I go on with my story?'

'Get on with it,' Fanny said. She was finding it hard to get much speed out of her little car on the twisting road.

'Then I took action,' Gaylord said. 'I packed up that goddam stool and the sketchpad and I went out into the main street and took a cab—after going round the back to check it had a licence number—and I went to that square where you park your car—'

'Myddleton Square,' Fanny prompted.

'Well, I didn't know that at the time, but the cab driver was a most obliging fellow and I sort of described the way once we got to your flat. Then I drove down here to look for you.'

'I must admit you did well to find us,' Sir Stafford said. 'Was it just blind luck?'

'I made a systematic search,' Gaylord said. 'A verbal search in a nice little bar I found. One of the scouts I recruited said that as I am an American I should go and see the airbase the Yanks used in War. I thought a deserted airbase was exactly where a dim-witted thug of a cab driver would take a dark-haired captive beauty to have his wicked way. So I went there. I was driving around when I found you.'

'Lucky for us,' Fanny said, and smiled. He seemed to her to leave out more than he told them, but now, she thought, was not the time or place to question him.

'Indeed,' Sir Stafford said in his croaking old man's voice, 'a tale of extraordinary persistence.' But then Sir Stafford said, 'He's catching up!'

Fanny saw the lights of the pursuer looming large in the driving mirror.

She knew the road. There was a long straight stretch coming up, the river lay behind willows on the left. Then the road turned across a narrow bridge where she would have to slow. She pushed the accelerator to the floor. She must get as far ahead as she could before the corner.

The pursuing lights came closer. She was doing 70 mph, but seemed to be standing still.

The vehicle behind pulled out to pass. Fanny braked, afraid he was trying to sideswipe her.

The car passed and accelerated away; it was a car nothing like the Millwall supporter's London taxi.

Fanny's nearside wheels touched the edge of the road. The tarmac had broken away. There was a gully between the road and a narrow strip of river bank where fishermen parked at weekends. Fanny fought to get back on to the road, but she was going too fast and the camber was too strong.

As though in slow motion the car lurched and slid gently to rest in a small bay of thick mud.

'I'm sorry,' Fanny said. 'There was nothing I could do.'

'It could've been worse,' Sir Stafford said.

'You're getting blasé,' Gaylord said to him, 'your second car crash in a week.'

'I'll have you know I've never been in a car crash in my life, young man,' Sir Stafford said.

'We've got to get out of here,' Fanny said. 'There's a pub called The Mulberry Bush a bit further on.'

She pushed the door open and stepped out into cold slime.

'Dammit,' Gaylord said, 'I'm wearing my white buckskin shoes.' He lifted the old man out and carried him to dry ground. He set him down beside the twisted roots of a fallen willow.

'Make yourself comfortable,' he said. 'Fanny and I'll be back as soon as we can.'

'What are you thinking of? We can't leave him,' Fanny said.

'You go ahead,' Sir Stafford said. 'I'd slow you up. Go on, hurry.'

'No,' Fanny said, 'it's too dangerous leaving you here alone. Help him up,' she said to

Gaylord.

Gaylord and Fanny set off up the road, helping Sir Stafford.

'That was stupid,' Fanny said. 'I should've known that couldn't be the taxi.'

'Think nothing of it. I expect they'll recover. It's only mud.'

'I didn't mean your shoes, for God's sake!'

'No,' Gaylord said sadly, 'I don't suppose you did.'

They walked on in silence. Fanny's feet slipped in her soaked shoes, and her skirt slapped against her bare legs. She was scarcely decent.

'There's a car coming,' Gaylord said.

Fanny pulled Sir Stafford off the road into the cover of the trees and ducked down, but Gaylord stepped out into the road in its path. 'Gee, we're in luck, it's a cab. Here, cabbie!'

'Come back,' Fanny shouted, but it was too late. The taxi slowed and stopped.

'Oh, my God,' Fanny said. She could see the Millwall supporter sitting at the wheel.

Gaylord walked to the driver's window and leaned in.

'Say,' he said, 'take me to the nearest police station, will you?'

Fanny, down in the wet grass with Sir Stafford, held her breath.

'Not for hire,' the driver said. He jabbed a finger upwards. 'Light's not on. I'm on my way home.'

Fanny realized the Millwall supporter did not connect the gangling American madman with Sir Stafford and herself.

'You've got to take me. There's been an accident,' Gaylord said.

'What accident?' His tone was nasty. The last thing he wanted to do was help citizens in trouble.

'A car's driven into the river. An old man and a girl. I tried to save them, but I couldn't get to them. I gotta get to the police and tell them.'

'Dead, was they?' A sort of kindness crept into the man's voice.

'I'm afraid so,' Gaylord said. 'They were swept away in the river.'

'Well, I don't want nothing to do with it,' the taxi driver said. He snapped the window shut, nearly trapping Gaylord's fingers.

'Hey!' Gaylord shouted, springing back. 'These fingers are insured for three million bucks.'

The taxi moved off. When it had gone, Gaylord shrugged. He offered Fanny his arm with exaggerated courtesy as she got up.

'That was brilliant, young man,' Sir Stafford said. 'I was in Intelligence in the War and we had agents who could think on their feet like that.'

'Feet?' Gaylord said. 'Look at mine. These shoes are ruined.'

Sir Stafford patted him on the back, but

Fanny knew Gaylord wasn't like the agents Sir Stafford had sent out into danger all those years ago. At least now I know what he did in the War if anyone else ever asks, she thought.

At the pub the bar was quiet. Two old men in a corner were using beermats on the top of a table to replay a local cricket game. A burly young farm worker with a ponytail was entwined with a spindly girl in a tight leopardskin skirt.

A big-bosomed barmaid tut-tutted over Fanny's bedraggled state.

'My shoes are ruined,' Gaylord said. 'You can wash the skirt and sew it up and no one will ever know the difference, but look at these shoes.'

'We need to call a cab,' Fanny said to the barmaid. 'We drove off the road.'

'I gotta get a drink,' Gaylord said.

'Oh, you're an American,' the barmaid said. She seemed to accept that this explained everything. 'Over here seeing the sights?' she asked.

'I'll say I am,' Gaylord said, looking down at her large bosom.

CHAPTER EIGHTEEN

Fanny rang for a taxi to come from Didcot, and then she made some effort to wash the worst of the mud off her legs and feet.

When she returned to the bar Sir Stafford was seated alongside the girl in the leopardskin skirt and Gaylord was showing the barmaid his white shoes.

'I've called a taxi, but it's some way for him to come,' Fanny told Sir Stafford.

Fanny took him a drink, then returned to Gaylord at the bar.

'I think we should leave him quiet for a while,' she said. She thought Gaylord might go over and start interrogating him. 'He's an old man and he looks exhausted.'

'I'm exhausted,' Gaylord said. 'But you never showed me such consideration!'

She rummaged in her shoulder bag and brought out her contacts book. 'I'd better ring about the car,' she said. 'It'll need a breakdown truck to deal with it.'

She found the number and went out to the telephone in the passage and told them where the car was.

As she put the phone down there was a crash from the bar as the main door was thrown open.

Fanny pressed back against the wall and peered round the wall to see what was happening. The Millwall supporter was framed in the doorway.

Fanny watched him cross the room to where Sir Stafford sat beside the courting couple. The Millwall supporter squeezed himself next to Sir Stafford, pushing the farmhand and his girl roughly aside. His hand was in his pocket and Fanny could see the outline of something that could be the barrel of a pistol.

The Millwall supporter ignored Gaylord. He had obviously put him down as a crazy Yank who had nothing to do with anything.

'I got a shooter,' he said to Sir Stafford. 'You come with me.'

But in jabbing the gun-barrel against Sir Stafford the thug drove his elbow quite hard against the farmhand's girlfriend.

She jumped to her feet.

'Get you dirty hands off me, you pervert,' she screeched. 'Justin, he touched me up.'

The burly Justin grabbed the Millwall supporter by the shoulders.

The girl shrieked. Tables and chairs crashed and shattered. Fanny went back to the telephone and dialled 999.

'There's a *riot* down at The Mulberry Bush pub on the Didcot Road,' she said, sounding breathless. 'They're *killing* each other. One man says he's got a gun.'

'What's your name?'

Fanny made a sound as like a hysterical woman as she could manage and put the phone down. Right, she said to herself, now to get Sir Stafford out of here.

The problem was solved for her. The street door opened and a man shouted, 'Taxi for Dinmont.'

Gaylord took her arm and they skirted the two brawling men to grab Sir Stafford, carrying him out like a bag of shopping between them.

There was a howl of rage from the Millwall supporter, but the burly Justin had him in a headlock; and the leopard-skirted girlfriend was delivering kicks with heavy lumpen-heeled boots.

The taxi was parked outside, the engine running.

'Rowfield,' Gaylord said to the driver. 'As fast as you can.'

On the main road they passed two squad cars with lights flashing and sirens wailing speeding towards The Mulberry Bush.

'It's amazing,' Sir Stafford's old man's voice piped up, 'you think life has passed, that there's no more excitement in anything, and then just when you think that, something happens and you realize it's all still going on out there, it's you who's withdrawn from it.'

CHAPTER NINETEEN

In the kitchen of the Manor House Gaylord poured whisky into tumblers. He swallowed the contents of one at a gulp and refilled it before handing one glass to Fanny and another to Sir Stafford.

Sir Stafford's hand was shaking as he drank.

His pin-striped suit hung creased and dirty. He looked exhausted, like a death's head.

Fanny felt light-headed after a small sip of whisky.

Gaylord was in pompous mode. 'I think the time has come for a few explanations,' he said. He sounded like Inspector Fulwell.

'I don't understand any of this,' Sir Stafford said. 'I'm grateful to you for rescuing me, of course, but I've been abducted and held prisoner and I can't understand why you haven't taken me straight to the nearest police station. They must be searching for me.'

'They *are* searching for you,' Gaylord said. 'They're searching for you as a dangerous driver who ran away from a fatal car accident.'

'You said something about a car crash before,' Sir Stafford said. 'What's all this about?'

'I'll tell him,' Fanny said. And she did.

When she finished, Sir Stafford sat in silence for a moment. Then he shook his head. 'I don't pretend to know what's going on,' he said. 'But I must be able to prove I wasn't in a car crash.'

Gaylord refilled their glasses. 'I wonder,' he said. 'It's obviously a set-up job. The lorry driver was George Miller. Your car crashed, your fingerprints were all over it, your assistant's body was in the passenger seat.'

'Poor Burroughs,' Sir Stafford said. 'I'm sorry about Burroughs.'

'What really happened?' Fanny asked. 'What's all this about?'

'I've no idea,' Sir Stafford said. 'The more I hear, the more confusing it all gets.'

'Tell us what happened to you that night?' Gaylord said. 'That may shed some light on this business.'

'It started with the icon,' Sir Stafford said.

'The icon?' Fanny could not help interrupting.

'Burroughs found an icon in his office,' Sir Stafford said.

'What do you mean, he found it?' Gaylord asked.

'As far as I could gather, he opened a cupboard and there it was,' Sir Stafford said.

'Then what did he do?'

'Well, I understand he'd noticed something of the sort on Ian Ramsey's wall, so he asked him about it. But Ian knew nothing. He said he didn't know anything about office decoration. Apparently Miss Field had done all that when he moved in. He presumed she'd got the pictures as a job lot somewhere.'

'And had she? He must've asked her.'

'Oh, yes. Burroughs thought that perhaps she was planning to put the thing up on his wall because one of his pictures was going away to be cleaned. He told her that if so he would rather have something less colourful. Burroughs was a religious man, a Nonconformist. He didn't really approve of graven images. But she'd never seen it, knew nothing about it. Burroughs said she was a bit shocked, she seemed to think he thought she'd got some kind of religious fetish. She said she'd only put the one on Ian Ramsey's wall because she'd found it among his golfing prints and assumed he wanted it there. She wouldn't have given it wall space. Thought it was some kind of evil omen.'

'So Mr Burroughs brought it to you?' Fanny asked.

'Yes. He thought it might be valuable, and wondered if it was mine. Burroughs knew I'm a bit of a collector of antiquities. It was a beautiful thing,' Sir Stafford added.

'And then?' Gaylord prompted him.

Sir Stafford continued in his exhausted old man's voice. 'I remembered the name of this chap in Rowfield who was something of an expert. Son of an old friend. He said he'd look at it. Burroughs and I were going down to my country house in Gloucestershire to work over the weekend so I said we'd drop it in. I warned him we'd be late, but he said he'd be there. Had a client to see at a restaurant in the village, something like that.'

'Where were you to meet?' Gaylord asked.

'He runs an antique business there, he said he'd be there. He has an office at the back.'

'And then?'

'Well, he never turned up. We found the place open and the lights blazing, but when we went in and looked around, he wasn't there.'

'That's a bit dangerous, isn't it? Leaving a place like that unlocked?' Gaylord and Fanny exchanged glances. They were trying to remember what Piers had said about being called away to The Bull.

'I thought so.'

'So there you are, icon in hand. What happened then?' Gaylord asked.

'I'm not sure. The lights went off, and someone grabbed me from behind. I thought he was going to pull the head off my body. When the lights came on, Burroughs wasn't there. But these men were, the men from Copsey, they tied me up and put something in my mouth to gag me.'

Gaylord brought the whisky bottle across to Sir Stafford and poured another tot into the old man's glass.

'Try to remember,' he said, 'did you hear anything? Did they mention a name, or a place, or anything at all?'

'One of them made a call on a mobile phone. I heard him say one had got away but they'd got the main item. I thought he meant the icon. I thought they were stealing that. I didn't connect it with Burroughs. And then the one who'd been on the phone said to the other "You know what to do" and he nodded and picked up a candlestick on the desk and went off.'

'And then?' Gaylord asked the old man.

'They put something over my face, and the next thing I knew, I woke up in that hovel where Fanny found me.' He looked at Fanny. 'They didn't mean the icon, did they? Poor Burroughs, he didn't get away.'

'No,' Gaylord said, 'they killed him with that brass candlestick.'

'In my cottage,' Fanny said.

She imagined poor Mr Burroughs running out into the lane behind Bentham's and out into the High Street. The Bull was closed, there was no one about for him to turn to.

'He tried to find me,' she said. 'He knew I had a cottage there. And he knew I had icons. I'd told him about them. I told him how I go in through The Bull's car park. But they were after him.'

She turned to Sir Stafford. 'He got to my place and I wasn't there. I hadn't arrived. If I had been there, I wonder what I could have done?'

She was about to add that Burroughs had left the icon in her cottage, but Gaylord gave her a warning look. He said to Sir Stafford, 'It's a fantastic story. Too fantastic for the police. They've already got Fanny taped as a dangerous lunatic.'

'And drunk, thanks to you,' she said.

'But how did Burroughs get in? Surely your cottage was locked?' Sir Stafford said.

'This is the country,' she said. 'I suppose I didn't lock the door.'

Gaylord interrupted, saying, 'It can't have been just the icon they were after, can it, Sir Stafford, or why didn't they kill you? They wanted you alive. Why didn't you turn up dead behind the driving wheel of your car with Mr Burroughs?'

'Gaylord!' Fanny felt she had to protect the old man. Gaylord sounded suddenly ruthless.

Sir Stafford shook his head. 'I don't know,' he said.

'I don't mean to be rude,' Gaylord persisted, 'but what does anyone gain from keeping you alive? What have you got that they want?'

'Money? It always comes down to money. Maybe a ransom,' Sir Stafford said.

Gaylord considered this and then shook his head.

'I don't think it's anything so simple. Why go to the trouble of telling the world you'd gone missing but you weren't dead? It was quite an elaborate story. There must be something else?'

'Power, I suppose. Influence. They may have wanted to make me do something to their advantage. Something political, do you think?'

From the way Sir Stafford was coming up with answers to Gaylord's question, Fanny realized that he had already given the subject a lot of thought. He must have been wondering the same thing himself all those hours he spent imprisoned in that sordid Copsey kitchen.

'Or,' Gaylord said, 'they wanted to use your

absence to do something you would never approve. Something you couldn't change when you returned.'

'They wouldn't have to keep him alive for that,' Fanny said. 'It's as though they were going to make decisions while you were on leave and pretend you were making them yourself, Sir Stafford. Who could do that? Who makes the decisions in your absence?'

Fanny already knew the answer to that but she wanted to hear Sir Stafford say it.

'Well, Ian Ramsey is my deputy. I suppose he would.' Sir Stafford gave a tired smile. 'It hasn't arisen before. I'm never absent.'

'But,' Fanny said, 'wouldn't Ian Ramsey be better off if you were dead? He'd take over the company then.'

She was thinking that Ian Ramsey had given her the Copsey address, sent her off in the taxi with the Millwall supporter. He had received the letter purporting to be from Sir Stafford, he was the one who had identified the writing as Sir Stafford's.

Sir Stafford looked up at them. 'No, actually,' he said, 'it wouldn't help him at all if I were dead. My death will not give Ramsey control of my company.'

Fanny saw the old man swell with pride as he said these words.

'Can you be sure of that?' she asked.

'Yes, I'm quite sure. I have other plans. My point is, Ian won't take over. He'll stay with the company, but he won't have any more power than at present. Which isn't much, after all.'

There was something cruel about the way Sir Stafford said this. Fanny realized that over the last few hours she had come to see Sir Stafford as a frail and abused old man at the end of his tether. He was nothing of the sort.

'So the point is,' Gaylord said, 'this Ian Ramsey's only chance of a taste of real power is when you, Sir Stafford, are merely *hors de combat* and not dead. I guess we don't have to look much further for the perpetrator in the case.'

Fanny was quite ready to think Ian Ramsey guilty, but this scheme seemed excessively elaborate.

'Why would he kill Mr Burroughs?' she protested. 'And where do the icons come into it?'

Gaylord said:

'Maybe Burroughs' death was an accident. When it happened, this Ian Ramsey had to think on his feet. How to get rid of the inconvenient body and make sure Sir Stafford is kept out of the office for a nice long time so that he can practise running a big business. Long enough, anyway, to look good on his CV when he has to look for a new position after Sir Stafford's *real* death.'

'I can't allow this, even in jest,' Sir Stafford

said. 'Ian Ramsey is the last person . . . I trust him implicitly. It is out of the question that he could be implicated in this preposterous affair.'

There was an awkward silence. Fanny got to her feet.

'It's no good,' she said. 'I've got to have a cup of tea.'

Gaylord pointed at a cupboard where he kept teabags. Then he said, 'The icon is the key to this. There's something about that icon that someone in your company, Ian Ramsey or A.N.Other, was afraid you'd discover if an expert saw it.'

'And if it was Ian Ramsey,' Fanny said, 'it's not too far-fetched to assume that whatever the secret of the icon is, that's why he needed to get Sir Stafford out of the way and be in charge of the company himself.'

The kettle boiled and she made the tea.

'It is much too far-fetched for me,' Sir Stafford said.

Fanny, sipping tea, looked round the kitchen. Her eyes rested on the shabby armchairs, the table that looked like a butcher's chopping block, the yellowing stove in the inglenook with the empty dogs' baskets on either side. And then she looked across at the old man sitting there with a mug of tea and reflected that he was one of the richest men in the world. He probably hadn't been in a kitchen in decades.

And there was Gaylord, swigging whisky, his long legs stretched out in front of him, Gaylord whom she had only met a few nights ago and was now like an old friend. Also a lover, the first real lover since Alan.

And that seemed at least as far-fetched to her as anything Ian Ramsey might have done at TROD.

CHAPTER TWENTY

In the morning Fanny planned to set off for London with Sir Stafford. After a night's sleep, Sir Stafford declared himself physically fit, but he would not, he said, go into the office today. 'Keep 'em guessing,' he said. 'You can keep your eyes open for anything unusual, Fanny. Someone will expect me to be back at work today.'

Fanny said, 'Can I borrow your car, Gaylord?'

'You mean Harry's prize possession?' Gaylord looked doubtful. 'Try to avoid rivers, ponds, boating lakes and big puddles,' he said. 'Are you sure it's a good idea?'

'I'll drive carefully.'

'No, I mean going to the office.'

'I told Miss Field I'd be in,' Fanny said. 'If it's Ian Ramsey behind all this, he doesn't know I know he knows. It'll look better if I behave as though I don't connect him with anything that happened. See how he reacts.'

'You're mad,' Gaylord said. 'But do what you like.'

He gave her a set of the Buick's keys and led her outside to show her how the car worked.

She said, 'Gaylord, why did you stop me mentioning that Burroughs left the icon in the cottage?'

'Because I don't trust the old boy,' Gaylord said. 'He's a mogul. He could have set this whole thing up playing some mogul game of his own, but it went wrong and now he's trying to cover himself.'

'Don't be daft,' Fanny said. 'He's the victim. Or one of them, anyway.'

'Sure,' Gaylord said. 'Did you ever think maybe old Burroughs was running away from Sir Stafford when he got himself killed? Remember, Sir Stafford isn't the feeble old gent he looks. And he was a spymaster in the War. Maybe he was trying to relive those glorious days and it went wrong.'

But then Sir Stafford came out, ready to go. He looked pale and his clothes were in bad shape, but he was once again clearly a force to be reckoned with. In the car, he made it obvious that he was only too pleased to get away from Gaylord. 'I don't trust that fellow,' he told Fanny. 'He doesn't take anything seriously.'

Fanny wanted to say that that was what she liked about Gaylord. It was what made him so refreshingly different from Alan, who took everything in deadly earnest. But she didn't say anything.

It was another beautiful late summer morning. The villages she drove through had not yet woken to the day. She looked in passing at the thatched cottages with their still-drawn curtains and the sleepy streets of yellow stone basking in the sunshine, at the patient cows gathered in the farmyards waiting to be milked, and the sparkling, dancing river she could not believe was the same murky leaden Thames that flowed through London. It was hard to believe the events of yesterday in such a peaceful setting. She was sorry when she reached the motorway.

The traffic was heavy. She had to concentrate on driving the big left-hand drive American car. It was no wonder Gaylord had difficulty knowing his right from his left when he was driving in England. Sir Stafford sat quietly reading the *Financial Times* which Fanny had stopped to buy for him at a petrol station.

'You can't rely on anything these days,' he said suddenly. 'Listen to this.'

He read out a story about a small African country Fanny had never heard of, which just happened to have some of the world's most important titanium deposits. 'There's been a coup, a bloody civil war, and the mining has stopped. In no time the world price will hit the roof, and someone will have made a fortune.'

'But who?' Fanny asked.

'Whoever fomented the coup in the first place, of course,' Sir Stafford said.

'You mean an outside country? Or a crazy dictator?'

'No. I mean international business interests,' Sir Stafford said.

'But that's appalling,' Fanny said. 'Thousands of people will die in the fighting. And think of the refugees . . .'

But Sir Stafford had turned the page of the newspaper and was reading the market reports. Fanny looked at his absorbed face. She wondered if what Sir Stafford called international business interests could include the interests of TROD.

At the moment Sir Stafford didn't look much like a cruel and wicked exploiter of the innocent. Fanny thought, he looks like a tramp. If he's not careful, they'll call the police when he tries to get into his flat.

But Sir Stafford didn't have any trouble going home. 'I won't forget what you've done,' he said. For a moment Fanny could see him briefing agents before they parachuted behind enemy lines.

She drove on to Clerkenwell. London looked rather sparkling, as good in its own way as the peaceful Oxfordshire countryside; it was hard to believe that it might harbour people who would deliberately foment revolution, death and starvation in order to make money.

She parked the old Buick on a meter near her flat. It was an awkward car to manoeuvre. She thought about Gaylord's friend, the mysterious Harry Hughes. She wondered if he had made his millions by making far-off people have civil war. Like everybody else she'd seen the pictures of the refugee camps and the starved, dying children too weak to brush the flies from their staring eyes, and she wondered if such scenes were the cost of the shiny old Buick.

She locked the car and went home and changed into a severe dark skirt and plain cotton shirt. For some reason, perhaps because he was an advocate of 'method dressing', she thought of Alan as she rode in a taxi to the office. She hadn't seen the ex for some time. She wondered what he was up to, if Miss America was still on, and how he was doing at work, whatever that work was. Like Gaylord's Harry Hughes, Alan Dinmont was a man of mystery too. She wasn't sure he was honest. Of course he wasn't in the big league, but he was ambitious. If Alan had the chance, he wouldn't be troubled by his conscience.

It seemed to Fanny, when she reached the TROD building in its serene time warp, that the tranquil cul-de-sac no longer looked so peaceful. This, too, had been paid for by blood money of a sort, not perhaps by the mass starvation of children, but everyone involved in its getting and making paid a high price in terms of stress and fear and nervous pressure.

As soon as she got into the office, she had a good example right there. Miss Field, her face set with constant worry about money for her mother and the aunt in Clapham, was already at her desk. As Fanny walked past the open door, Miss Field called out, 'Who's that?' Her voice was tentative. 'Mrs Dinmont, is that you?'

Today's blouse was yellow, also with a big floppy bow. It did not suit Miss Field any better than the others. Her face glowed an unhealthy pale shade of the jaundiced material.

'I didn't expect you in,' Miss Field said.

'Really, Miss Field? I can't think why not. Any coffee on the go?'

Fanny went into her office. Some start to my sleuthing career, she said to herself, I'm supposed to suspect everybody and the first thing I do is give the secretary the opportunity to put poison in the coffee.

When Miss Field came in with the coffee Fanny said, 'Why didn't you expect me in, Miss Field? I told you I would be.'

Miss Field changed colour, from dough to baked cake.

'Mr Ramsey said not to expect you,' she said.

Oh, he did, did he? Fanny thought. 'Is Mr Ramsey in?' she asked Miss Field.

Miss Field nodded and Fanny thought there was something peculiar beside the colour of her blouse about Miss Field today. This was the woman who had cried 'an evil omen' when confronted with the mystery icon. Maybe she had always been peculiar. Then maybe she had gone peculiar in Sir Stafford's service. Sir Stafford himself was peculiar. Ian Ramsey, indeed, seemed quite normal. It was perhaps the golf that gave him the stamp of normality.

'Yes,' Miss Field said, in that weird strained office voice of hers, 'Mr Ramsey is in.'

Fanny felt guilty not to stop and chat a bit with Miss Field, giving the poor old thing a chance to talk. There was nothing dramatic like a revolution about Miss Field's situation, but it filled her life even if it was a modest little everyday martyrdom.

Fanny went across the landing to Ian Ramsey's office. If he was the villain, she wanted to see how he reacted to her appearance. She knocked as she opened his door.

'Good morning,' she said.

His first reaction was to take off the spectacles he had been wearing to practise his putting on the green of the office carpet. Fanny could understand why he disliked being seen wearing them. They made his pale moonstone eyes look like flawed glass. No, Ian

Ramsey wasn't that normal either. He looked like a man with two glass eyes. Suddenly the putter in his hand looked an awful lot like what those turners of nifty phrases in police reports call a blunt instrument. She wondered if he would cry Fore! before he struck.

'Well, Fanny, I was sure you'd take the morning off. You're very conscientious.'

'Copsey is only fifty miles or so from London, Ian,' she said. 'People even commute to work every day from my sleepy hamlet on Thames. I hardly need a holiday to recover from that.'

The light caught what might be beads of sweat on Ian Ramsey's nose and upper lip. Fanny, watching him for signs of fear or fury, was not sure. With those little beads of moisture he looked as though he was on the boil.

'Well, what have you to report?' he asked, putting his golf club away and throwing himself into one of the leather deckchairs.

'What about?'

'My dear girl, wake up! About Miller the lorry driver, of course. What did he have to say? How did it go?'

'I don't know,' she said, 'I never saw him.'

'What! Well, that was a wasted journey! Good heavens.'

'Yes, I'm afraid it was,' Fanny said. 'I got there and the house seemed empty, but the door was open and while I was looking I managed to shut myself in a lavatory.'

Fanny smiled one of those empty-headed little dolly smiles that always go down well with the more oinking variety of male chauvinist pig.

'Did you indeed?' Ian Ramsey said. 'Ha! ha! ha!'

Or maybe it was more ho! ho! ho!, Fanny thought. It was avuncular, anyway.

'Mr Ramsey—Ian—I'm not sure, but I think someone locked me in deliberately. I didn't see anyone, and I suppose the door might've stuck and I panicked, but . . . It was awful. The lavatory had a ceiling about twenty foot high. I had to sort of shimmy up the walls. I got out through a skylight.'

She bent down to examine one knee cap.

'I ruined my stockings. And a good dress.'

'Poor Fanny,' he said. He gave her the smile that made him good-looking. 'But what a fit person you must be,' he said.

He was looking at her with curiosity, but she could not be sure what he was thinking. Maybe he was going to ask her if she played golf.

'There could be some mistake about the address,' she said. 'I can't believe that Mr Miller really lives in that awful place.'

'Well, it doesn't really matter any more,' Ramsey said. 'Of course, you haven't heard our news. We've heard from Sir Stafford. He's coming back to the office tomorrow.'

She made sure her eyes did not waver, in

case he was watching her for a reaction.

'That's wonderful!' she said. 'Is he all right?'

'That remains to be seen.'

She wondered if she was imagining the hint of a threat.

'What happened? What does he say?' she asked.

'He didn't say much at all.'

Ramsey got to his feet and walked heavily to the window. He kept his back turned to Fanny. Maybe he was doing that so she couldn't see the disappointment on his face. Or maybe he was examining the good golfing weather out there. Finally he said, 'Apparently Sir Stafford turned up at his flat early this morning looking like a tramp. He remembers absolutely nothing about what happened.'

'It'll probably come back to him gradually.'

Fanny knew that sounded like a challenge; she meant it to.

'D'you think so?' Ramsey turned to her, his back now against the light from the window. 'I don't know much about these things.'

'I believe they have ways of helping people remember now.'

'I wonder if he'll remember hiring you?' Ian Ramsey said.

CHAPTER TWENTY-ONE

Sir Stafford was in the office next morning. Miss Field came running out on the landing as Fanny came up the stairs. Her blouse today was baby blue, and she wore a sapphire pin at her throat, a good one, not glass. That morning the faded secretary was blooming like a neglected pot plant suddenly watered. The excitement had evidently dispelled thoughts of the house in Clapham, at least for the morning.

'He's here,' she said. Her voice had lost twenty years. 'He's back. Everything will be all right now'

Miss Field had a telephone message for Fanny from Percy Parfitt. It was mysteriously simple: 'What price Ethiopia?' Just that and nothing more.

'Is that all he said?' Fanny asked.

Miss Field seemed puzzled.

'It didn't make any sense to me,' she said. 'He said you'd know what he meant.'

Fanny didn't want Miss Field to think she was implying any criticism of her efficiency.

'I do know. It's just that I thought he might've said a bit more.' She smiled at Miss Field and Miss Field smiled back, and Fanny realized that today Miss Field was not the self-doubting creature she had been without Sir Stafford. That was perfectly logical. Without Sir Stafford, Miss Field's job wasn't secure. Fanny couldn't see Ian Ramsey, or anyone like him, keeping Miss Field on once Sir Stafford was gone. They'd want someone young and attractive. But Miss Field didn't need her job just for herself, she had the mother and aunt to support, and Sir Stafford was an old man, he wouldn't go on for many more years, and then . . . It was no wonder Miss Field was the way she was.

Fanny was about to ring Percy Parfitt when Sir Stafford called her into his room. She saw Ian Ramsey open his door as she crossed the landing. Even in the discreet lighting Fanny could see he was sweating more than usual. He looked like something simmering on a stove.

But he managed a smile.

'Sir Stafford probably wants to know who you are and what the hell you're doing sitting at old Burroughs' desk,' he said.

'There's dandruff on your shoulders,' Fanny said, determined to give as good as she got.

It was the first time she had been in Sir Stafford's inner sanctum. It opened on to the small faceless conference room where he had interviewed her for the job. But she recognized his office as the natural habitat of the wizard. It was dark and stately, with heavy furniture and framed photographs showing Sir Stafford with the famous, a member of the Royal family at Ascot; Sir Stafford in three separate photographs with three separate American Presidents; Sir Stafford among a smiling group of European heads of state. The panelled walls were hung with more photographs, of faded massed schoolboys and college groups. Fanny noticed one of an Oxford University eight. It seemed odd to her that a man of his slight physique should have been interested in rowing. Then she recognized him. Of course, he was the cox. There was a photo of him with Tony Blair and one from a decade earlier with a smiling Margaret Thatcher.

Sir Stafford got up from behind his desk and came over to shake hands with her. Fanny was embarrassed. In her torn clothes and half-naked she had carried this old man through blackthorn hedges, ducked into thickets hiding from the bad guys, driven him into a river on a wild chase and drunk whisky with him half the night before going upstairs to bed with her lover. But the way Sir Stafford was now, none of these things might have happened. Sir Stafford might have been a complete stranger.

The old man wore an immaculate suit in dark pinstripe worsted, an exact replica of the one that had been ruined yesterday. Looking at him, Fanny thought what a difference presentation made. What had been a frail old man in a ragged suit was a thing of steel in a clean one.

'I believe you've done some sterling work for us these last few trying days,' he said.

He didn't smile; he didn't give her a nod or a nudge; he certainly did not wink.

'I was only doing my job,' she said. She sounded cold. 'I've got to talk to you,' she added. 'I wonder, does TROD have active interests in Ethiopia?'

'Ethiopia? What a strange question, why do you ask? One of Mr Poyntz's theories, is it? We did get involved, as a matter of fact, but that was before the coup. Ian knows about that, it was his pigeon. He went out there, I remember. I still tend to think of it as Abyssinia. That's how old I am!'

Fanny could tell he was quite proud of being so out of date.

Sir Stafford droned on to her, thanking her for her efforts on behalf of the company. At least, she thought, he hasn't forgotten he hired me. I've still got a job.

Then he said, 'I like your costume.' His expression was deadpan.

Fanny laughed. She couldn't help it, but Sir Stafford remained poker-faced. She hadn't really thought he had noticed the state she'd been in when she rescued him, but he had. But then, men in his position didn't miss things.

She went back to her office. Three times she tried to reach Percy Parfitt to ask about his cryptic message, but he was not available. She found it hard to concentrate. She kept thinking of Gaylord. She tried not to, but his image kept appearing. At least, she thought, it's a change from forcing myself not to think about Alan. Even when she brought Alan to mind, she could only wonder what he would have had to say if he'd seen her bowling up the motorway at the wheel of a great big American car.

She dragged her mind off Gaylord and rang Percy Parfitt again. He was in this time and he was excited. The icon was Ethiopian, just as he thought, a Crusader icon made by a French artist who had set up an atelier and worked there. Percy was particularly excited because although it was known from the Sinai collection that icons were brought from outside to St Catherine's monastery as gifts, Mr Burroughs' icon was the first definite evidence of a European maker's atelier so far from the centre of the Crusaders' empire.

Fanny was interested and excited by what Percy Parfitt said, but the news seemed to make the icon seem remote from her. It's nothing to do with me any more, she thought, it'll go to the British Museum or something and that'll be that. The icon was always too rare a thing for her, and now it had historical importance, removing it from the ordinary world. She wasn't happy about that. For a short time the rare and wonderful thing had been hers, to keep and cherish. Or to sell. There was that, too. She felt guilty thinking about that, but she still thought about it.

That evening she walked home to try to

break out of her mood.

As she came to her own front door she noticed that the light was on in her sitting-room. Had she left it on when she went out? She remembered Gaylord warning her to be careful. Was George Miller or the Millwall supporter lying in wait for her? She stopped fretting about the lost icon and was afraid.

From the pavement she tried to see into the room. It looked rather cosy, with the books and pictures and the bulging old sofa. There was no sign of anything sinister. Everything seemed as she had left it.

Then she saw Gaylord come into the room from the hall. He was carrying a glass, of course. He did not look across to the window. He sat on the sofa, hunched forward peering at something on the floor.

Fanny felt suddenly happy. She unlocked the flat door and pretended surprise to see him.

'I'd forgotten you'd still got my keys,' she said. 'How did you get here?'

'You don't mind, do you? I couldn't very well sit out on the step. Not with all those people walking by giving me funny looks. Your car was ready, so I brought it up. You were lucky, it got going without much trouble.'

'What's that?'

She pointed to the pile of sketches on the floor by the sofa. The drawing on the top, the one he had been looking at, showed a young girl with curly hair and merry eyes.

'They're the sketches I drew of people who went into your office.'

'Yeah, and a few nubile young girls who had nothing to do with TROD at all,' Fanny said. 'I've got news for you. Percy Parfitt rang. The icon is Ethiopian. He's terrifically excited. Apparently it's even more rare and wonderful than he thought.'

Gaylord began searching his pockets for something. 'That reminds me,' he said, 'why I came. God, where is it? It's here somewhere. I put it in a safe place.' He produced a folded sheet of paper and handed it to her.

'Look at that,' he said.

Fanny opened the paper and stared at a list of names.

'There's some mistake,' she said. 'Is this a list of favourite cocktails?'

'Goddamit, didn't you ever learn geography?'

'OK, I know some of these are small countries in the Third World. Most of them are in the Third World, aren't they?'

'Yes they're all countries rich in some sort of mineral deposits, all in great demand among the industrialised nations for their chemical, scientific properties etc. etc . . .' he intoned like a man reading from a guide book.

'And?'

'These little dots on the map have something else in common, you will be surprised to hear. Apart from starving children and no mod cons.'

'Political instability?' Fanny said. 'And TROD?'

Gaylord's face fell. 'How did you know that? It took me hours to look it all up in the library.'

'Lucky guess. Go on.'

'They've all had revolutions in the last five years or so, that's all.'

'And TROD still reigns triumphant?'

Fanny asked.

'We'll have to check on that. That's why I came straight up here.'

'Are you thinking what I'm thinking?'

'Probably not, or you'd have filled my glass by now.' He got up and poured whisky sloppily into the tumbler.

'Gaylord, do these places have treasures, stuff like that?'

'Such stuff as dreams are made on? They sure do. That South American country has Conquistador gold, and that African one had so much platinum the women there once walked about using it for daywear.'

'So what we've got to find out is if someone from TROD got his fists on them when the coups came.'

'More than that,' Gaylord said slowly, 'TROD or someone there may well have played a more important part.' Fanny was shocked.

'Started the coups, you mean?'

'Why not?' Gaylord said. 'Take the icon. Ethiopia had a coup. A Marxist coup. Lots of rich non-Marxists wanting to get out but the currency isn't worth anything any more. So someone sells the national treasure to Mr X for the price of a ticket out. Or swaps it for some goddam thing, a tank of his own, maybe.'

Fanny stared at him. 'But—?'

'I know,' he said, 'I know the buts. But it's possible. And if it's true, they could be bringing the stuff in through Copsey.'

'Stuff? You mean the valuables?'

'It's possible. I checked on Copsey today.'

'You have been busy,' Fanny said. She couldn't disguise the surprise in her voice.

'The aviation authorities say there are no flights from there any more. So I asked in the village, and people there said they'd heard flights at night. They think it's the Americans back again and doing something secret.'

'But the authorities would know.'

'Not if a small aircraft simply touched down. You don't actually know anything about TROD. Or Sir Stafford. Maybe it's a hobby of his. Maybe he's reliving the great adventures of his youth.'

'I can see him enjoying something like that. But he's not a crook.'

'Most people wouldn't think it very crooked grabbing up art treasures in the Third World. If he was paying for them they wouldn't think it crooked at all.'

'But Mr Burroughs was murdered.'

'Maybe, as I said before, old Sir Stafford got carried away by the game.'

For a while they were both silent. A police siren shrieked in a nearby street. A lorry braked. A group of teenagers yelled abuse.

'If he isn't in on it, he's in danger,' Gaylord said.

'Whoever is behind it was forced to act when Burroughs started to ask questions about that icon. They thought the game was up.'

Fanny got to her feet. Gaylord's pile of sketches were still on the floor.

'I'm going to see Sir Stafford,' she said. 'I can't talk to him in the office. It's not safe.'

'He's probably safe as long as he keeps pretending his memory's blank,' Gaylord said, 'But are you safe with him? I wouldn't bet on it.'

CHAPTER TWENTY-TWO

Sir Stafford lived on a quiet street close to the north side of Hyde Park. He had a flat in a fairly new luxury block overlooking the perimeter road. There were huge bulbous windows at each corner of the building on every level, which gave it the appearance of a cruise liner at anchor on a green sea. In its own context it was an ugly building.

Fanny smiled at a uniformed security guard sitting at a desk behind a glass screen. She was relieved that Sir Stafford had some protection at least. But the man didn't smile back. He had the hostile stare of an immigration official.

'Is Sir Stafford expecting you?' he asked. There was a large book on the desk in front of him where names of acceptable visitors were carefully written along ruled lines. The numbers of the apartments they were destined for appeared in little boxes on the right of the page.

'No,' Fanny said.

'Then I'm afraid . . .' He turned away.

Fanny rapped on the glass. 'Call his apartment and tell Sir Stafford that Ms Dinmont wishes to see him,' she said.

'Mrs Dinmont?' the man said. He gazed down at his book. 'Sir Stafford is expecting you,' he said. 'Twelfth floor.' He pointed to the lifts down the hallway behind him.

Well, Fanny thought, Sir Stafford didn't get where he is today without the ability to foretell the future.

She rode up in the lift suddenly feeling very poor. When the doors opened at Sir Stafford's floor, a youngish butler dressed in formal black came forward to greet her. He bowed. He did not speak.

'Come along in, Fanny. I'm in here.' Sir Stafford's voice called to her through a door across the hall.

Fanny started getting the creeps. It was uncanny that Sir Stafford knew that she would come to call. She began to think that maybe Gaylord was right and Sir Stafford, old and frail as he was, might be behind whatever was going on that led to Mr Burroughs' death. Perhaps there had been a falling out. George Miller and the Millwall supporter weren't Sir Stafford's type. If he had somehow put himself in league with them there was bound to be a falling out.

I'm being silly, she told herself, I'm just nervous paying an unexpected call on a billion quid.

The silent butler followed her into the room. Sir Stafford was sitting by a fireplace. There was a huge blue hydrangea in a pot. When he stood up she heard the joints in his knees crack. The room was very warm.

Blue seemed to be Sir Stafford's favourite colour. He wore a dark-blue smoking jacket, a blue-striped shirt; the carpet underfoot was powder blue, the rotund furniture, wherever it was covered in cloth, was blue, and so were the curtains. They had not been drawn and the evening sky was an obliging cobalt turning to peacock. The curve of the big windows made the room seem part of the sky, looking down on the tops of trees and the yellow light of the lamps in the park.

Fanny wanted to say the visit had been a

mistake and turn and flee.

'Drink?' Sir Stafford asked.

Fanny shook her head. She was afraid that if she had a glass in her hand it would shake and spill on the blue carpet.

The butler brought Sir Stafford a glass of whisky on a silver tray. He returned to a side table and brought back ice, then soda. Sir Stafford took the glass and put it solemnly on a coaster on the table by his chair. He gave some slight sign Fanny missed and the butler left. She heard the faint click as he shut the door.

Fanny was still nervous, but it was hard to resist the almost mechanical slowing of pace in the old man's presence. Gaylord couldn't be right. A man like Sir Stafford, a venerable man, couldn't be involved in crime. But then she remembered him reading the *Financial Times* in the car and how clearly disappointed he had been at not being party to the coup in Africa that would make someone a fortune. Men like that were capable of anything. Who was to say that in his old age Sir Stafford wouldn't leave off robbing countries wholesale and take up a genteel hobby like plundering art treasures?

Sir Stafford looked tired. She didn't like to meet his eyes. His papery eyelids were so thin she was afraid of seeing the eyeball beneath. She looked down. There it was again, blue. His feet were hidden in monogrammed royal blue velvet slippers. She looked up and he was looking at her and their eyes met. His were the half-buried eyes of an old man and they were blue.

'There are some questions . . .' she said.

'You'd better ask them,' he said, without interest. 'But I don't think I'll know the answers.'

'Is it possible that someone in the company is using political unrest in various small countries to buy up national treasures cheap, and then bring them here to sell them off for a fortune?'

Sir Stafford said nothing. There seemed to be no expression on his face. It was as if he hadn't heard her.

She wanted to tell him about the icon. She had come here to do it, despite Gaylord's warning. But she was remembering that warning now. Once again she thought, what if Gaylord is right? Sir Stafford's a powerful man. He's got the money and the power to play out his fantasies.

She took a deep breath. She had to tell him.

'It was the icon, you see,' she said. 'The night Mr Burroughs was killed he left the icon in my cottage. We—I—took it to an expert and he got very excited because apparently it's very rare and has been hidden away in an Ethiopian Coptic church all these years.'

'Well,' Sir Stafford said, 'that's very exciting, my dear, but—'

'Don't you see?' Fanny said. 'It was part of their national cultural heritage, the heritage that the Marxists broke up when they came to power.'

'I still don't see . . . it's a bit of a leap, you know.'

'Except it looks as though it's happened before. I'm sorry, Sir Stafford, but I think—we think—TROD's been playing both sides against the middle in several Third World countries with valuable natural resources, stirring up political unrest and supporting both sides.'

'So the company is in a position of strength whichever group comes out on top? But my dear girl, that's perfectly normal business practice, isn't it? We have to protect our interests.'

Fanny opened her mouth to argue, but then closed it. Sir Stafford was smiling at her.

She had to say something. She was the company's public relations person. It was her job now to protect TROD's good name, even if it didn't have one. 'But I'm talking about the company's interests,' she said. 'Someone in a position to do it has been taking advantage of the trouble in these places to get their hands on the art treasures. That isn't in the company's interests, is it? Someone is making a lot of money, flogging these things to private buyers over here. If they were going to museums or art galleries where the public could see them, at least there'd be some kudos for the company name. Like the Elgin Marbles.' That seemed an unfortunate comparison, and Fanny ended lamely, 'I think, anyway.'

Sir Stafford smiled. 'You didn't mention finding an icon in your cottage before this,' he said. 'Was that because you thought I was your villain?'

'It did seem a possibility for a while.'

'So you thought I'd killed old Burroughs to keep him from blowing the gaff?' Sir Stafford chuckled. He seemed rather flattered that she could have imagined such a thing.

'But then it was obvious someone wanted you out of the way so you wouldn't query some important company decisions. There's something going on that you would veto if you were in the office. At least, that's what we—Gaylord and I—think.'

Sir Stafford picked up his drink and sipped in slow motion. 'You think it's Ian Ramsey, I presume? You think he's the villain.'

It was not a question. Fanny said nothing.

'I've known him for years,' Sir Stafford said. 'Ever since he was a child. Before he played golf, even.' It was a joke. Fanny laughed. It was worth remembering always to laugh at great men's jokes.

'And you don't believe it?'

'I knew his father. A weak man, I suppose you'd call him. The mother, a beautiful woman and strong, ran everything. She loved Ian, he was her favourite, her younger son.'

'Has he got a brother?' Fanny was surprised. She had put Ian Ramsey down as a man whose siblings, if he had any, would be sisters.

'The older son was quite different. Always in trouble. Everyone loved him, but he didn't give a fig for anyone. Ian went into the family business with his father; it was shipping. And then the old man died and left everything to the older son, who'd never worked. I suppose the old man knew Ian would always be all right, so he left everything to the . . .'

The old man sought the right word '. . . the prodigal,' he said. 'It didn't do him much good, ran through it in no time. Then the beautiful mother died.'

Fanny wondered if she was raising the ghost of an old love affair between that beautiful woman and Sir Stafford. But even then Sir Stafford must have been an old man.

'How come you got Ian Ramsey into TROD?' she asked.

'He worked for us abroad for years. He did good work. I brought him back as my deputy.'

'Is he interested in art?' Fanny asked.

Sir Stafford paused. 'No, not at all. He collects what other people want. Not for himself. His mother was the same way. He wants other people to want them. You'll have to read what you can into that.'

She got up to go. 'Thank you, Sir Stafford,'

she said. 'Don't get up. I'll see you in the office.'

Looking down at him she thought again how old he was, an antique polished and cared for, but in danger of crumbling in contact with the polluted atmosphere of the modern world. It seemed to her for a moment that she was looking into the display cabinet of a taxidermist.

But then he said, 'You do realize, don't you, my unexpected return to the office may force a change of plan on our villain or villains?'

'They'll have to move fast, you mean?'

'I should think so,' Sir Stafford said. 'Don't you?'

Again Fanny wondered if she were not out of her league, playing a game with an opponent who knew what she was going to do before she had even thought to do it herself. But that was ridiculous. Sir Stafford had been abducted and imprisoned in that house in Copsey. Even now he was wanted by the police in connection with a fatal car crash. Or was he? Sir Stafford had been too calm and at ease in his blue room. Something had been done to keep the cops away from him. I've entered a mysterious world, Fanny thought, as shadowy as a Renaissance Borgia court.

She wished now that she had taken that drink, and that she'd told the butler to make it a large one.

CHAPTER TWENTY-THREE

Gaylord was still lounging on the settee where she had left him. She wondered if he had moved at all.

'Well?' he asked. 'Is all revealed? I've been thinking. Maybe we've got it all wrong and actually it's the high priests of the temple who have come to kill everybody for stealing the sacred icon.'

Fanny could see the second bottle on the floor at his feet.

'Without a doubt,' Gaylord said. 'I'm going for the priests from the temple theory.'

'Do be serious,' Fanny said.

'Which reminds me,' Gaylord said in a dignified voice, 'you'd better cast your eyes over the sketches I did outside TROD. After all, I came all this way to show them to you. And give you the benefit of my research on your behalf.'

Gaylord picked up the drawings at his feet and gave them to her.

She smiled at the sketches of sexy girls Gaylord had caught passing by in a few lines of wiggles and bosoms. Then she caught her breath.

Gaylord's sure pencil left no room for ambiguity. Gaylord had captured everything; the high-domed head that had once been thick brown curls and was now balding; the thickening of the former demon-lover hips, and, most cruel of all, the pleased self-satisfaction Fanny now saw revealed as the bravura show of a bully.

'What is it?' Gaylord asked. 'Who's that?'

'That's Alan,' she said. 'My ex-husband.'

'You don't say!'

'I do say, and more to the point, what was he doing there?'

'Visiting his newly employed old wife for a loan?'

'He must've been visiting Ian Ramsey. Alan knows him. That's what got me the job. Alan fixed it for me.'

'How cosy. Obviously you kids were made for each other. That's what he'd come to tell you.'

Fanny got to her feet and picked up the telephone.

'What are you doing?' Gaylord asked.

'I'm ringing Alan,' Fanny said.

'Gosh, the power of the artist! I feel real proud of myself. A quick sketch and you two are reconciled. I think you should call the firstborn Gaylord.'

'I'm going to ask him what the hell he was doing going into the TROD office.'

'Don't you think that's a bit direct? Shouldn't you try counselling first?'

Fanny dialled the number.

'Say,' Gaylord said, 'it's interesting that you

know the ex-hubby's number right off by heart. Doesn't that tell you something about yourself?'

'Shut up,' Fanny said as the phone was picked up the other end. 'Alan?' she said.

'Fanny?' Alan sounded astonished. And something else.

'I wanted to know . . . I heard you'd been into the TROD office while I was out. I wondered . . . were you looking for me? Did you want to see me?'

'Me? At the TROD office? Was I? No. The other day? Maybe I was. Why was that? Let's see, I can't talk here, not on the telephone.'

Fanny let him ramble. He was obviously nervous. That was what she had heard in his voice when he first picked up the phone, before he even knew it was an ex-wife on the line. And then she thought maybe it was something more than nervous. It was fear. It didn't make any sense.

'What's the matter, Alan? Is something wrong? Is it Miss America?'

'Who?'

'Tracy Thing, whatever her name is.'

'Oh, no. No. Well, yes, perhaps it's that.' She could hear him take a deep breath. 'Fanny, I can't talk now, but I need to talk to you. Could you come down here?'

'Alan, we're divorced. We're not even friends.'

'It's nothing to do with us,' he said. He

hesitated, then said in a rush, lowering his voice as though he did not want to be overheard, ‘It’s about your job, Fanny. About that company you work for.’

Fanny tried to exchange a significant look with Gaylord who, since he could not hear Alan’s voice, looked blank.

‘There’d better be a good reason, then,’ she said. ‘I know you, remember. That hasn’t changed.’

‘You know the address?’

‘Yes,’ she said. She knew the house in Ruislip, but she liked the idea of making him think she wasn’t sure. She hesitated over it as she repeated the street number. ‘That’s right, isn’t it?’

‘I always knew I could rely on you, Fan,’ Alan said, but he still sounded worried.

‘If it’s money, I haven’t got any,’ she said. ‘I’ll be with you by lunchtime tomorrow.’

There was a short silence. She put the phone down.

‘What did he want?’ Gaylord asked.

‘To see me.’

‘I told you, he’s seen the error of his ways, especially now you’re earning good money and he wants to start the reconciliation process by seducing you.’

‘It’s not like that.’

But what was it like then? She didn’t know. It wasn’t like Alan to be nervous, but then it wasn’t like him to live in Ruislip and be bald.

Something had gone seriously wrong with him and Fanny suspected that maybe it didn't have anything to do with Miss America.

'I could do with a drink,' she said.

Gaylord picked up a whisky bottle from the floor beside the settee and held it up. It was empty. 'So could I,' he said.

'Come to think of it, I'm starving. Let's go out and get something to eat.'

Upper Street was still crowded. A group of young men stood outside one of the pubs on Islington Green, singing snatches of Sixties pop songs. One of them lurched across the pavement towards Fanny swinging his hips and singing 'The Girl from Ipanima' with his arms held out as though inviting her to dance.

'Watch out,' one of his mates said, 'her grandad'll hit you with his bus pass.'

'Be missing,' Fanny said to the singer and he dropped his arms and moved away.

'What did you say to him?' Gaylord asked.

'Be missing.'

'Be missing? Is that all?'

'I said it with conviction.'

A much more sober group was emerging from the cinema. Fanny was thinking they all looked like Melanie Musgrove except they were smiling, then she heard her name called.

'Fanny, it's me, Melanie.'

Melanie was with a small group of women who placed themselves round her like bodyguards when she stopped in front of

Fanny and Gaylord.

'It's uncanny,' Melanie said, 'I'm hardly ever in London now and then on one of my rare visits I see you twice. We're practically next-door neighbours in the country and we don't see each other from one year's end to the next.'

She moved closer to Fanny. 'I saw the way you got rid of that thug,' she said, 'we could use you, Fanny. Some of those hunt supporters can get quite heavy.'

Melanie seemed to notice Gaylord for the first time. She adjusted her steel-rimmed spectacles and gave him a hard look with her small dark eyes, barely visible under her fringe.

'You're the man with the pets.' She said pets as if it were a dirty word.

'I am?' Gaylord was baffled.

'The dogs,' Melanie said.

'I'm looking after them for a friend.'

Gaylord was so apologetic Fanny had to smile.

'It's sick,' Melanie said, 'the whole idea of *pets.*' She turned to Fanny. 'You should help us,' she said, 'we need someone like you. Men are intimidated by you.'

Now it was Gaylord's turn to smile. Melanie failed to notice. She was still staring at Fanny.

'I'm working in London now,' Fanny said.

Melanie made a face. 'You're not in London at weekends, and we've got a big protest coming up on animal experiments. I'm looking for someone who can face up to those thugs. I'll be in touch.'

Gaylord took Fanny's arm and hustled her towards a steak restaurant.

'Quick,' he said, 'let's go in here. She wouldn't dare come in here after you.'

'There's a good Chinese further up,' Fanny said. 'I feel like Chinese, Melanie or no Melanie.'

'Anything you say, but what I don't understand is why you didn't tell her to be missing.'

'I couldn't do that,' Fanny said. 'After all, Melanie's been a useful contact and you never know when I might need her again.'

They went to a Thai restaurant and Gaylord drew amusing pictures of Melanie cornering timid little men who owned large and furious pets.

'Do I really intimidate men?' Fanny asked.

'Sure you do,' Gaylord said, barely glancing up from the drawing he was doing. 'You can bank on it.'

Somehow she couldn't see that as being much of an attraction.

CHAPTER TWENTY-FOUR

Fanny was late starting out for Ruislip, and then the traffic was moving slowly out of

London. Also she had to stop to make a telephone call. She had forgotten to ring Miss Field to say she would not be in the office until late afternoon, if at all. By that time she was quite hot and bothered. She sounded so agitated that Miss Field asked if everything was all right. It was a personal matter, Fanny said, she had to see her ex-husband. This is ridiculous, Fanny told herself, Alan and I are divorced, he's married again and I . . . I've got Gaylord. And that, she realized, was another reason why she was nervous—Gaylord was making seeing Alan again into some kind of test.

She had never been inside the house in Ruislip where Alan had moved with Miss America, but once she had driven past it, and it made her feel ashamed to think of that now. She hadn't been able to stop herself being curious; it was only natural but she hadn't liked giving in to it.

As she drove through leafy suburbs skirting golf courses and pony paddocks full of painted jumps, she found herself thinking that this was the sort of place Ian Ramsey might live. Perhaps it wasn't so surprising after all that he and Alan were apparently friends.

Fanny was driving the Buick. The old car would impress Miss America. It would certainly impress Alan, but, of course, as she told herself, that had nothing to do with it.

Alan's house, a detached red brick villa with

mock Tudor beams lacking any structural logic, was one of five on a sweeping close. A built-in double garage opened on a paved driveway, and beyond broad swathes of lawn a battalion of macrocarpa trees protected the house from sight of its neighbours.

The garage doors were open. Alan was putting something in the boot of a silver Mercedes. He shut the boot and came towards her, keys swinging from one finger. Gaylord had got him all right. He had more hair than in the drawing, but it was no longer the curly mane of her first love. And he was fatter. He wasn't Michelangelo's David any more, if he ever had been. Fanny supposed she'd been seeing differently in those days.

'What's funny?' he asked.

'Nothing,' she said.

'You're laughing.'

'Hello Alan.'

'You're so late I'd almost given you up,' he said. There was only one car in the garage.

'Isn't Tracy here?' Fanny asked.

She wondered if Miss America had run out rather than meet the ex-wife.

'We split up ages ago,' he said. Then he shrugged.

He was like a stranger. He was sleeker. He'd made some money, was making more. His voice seemed louder. His smile was a little . . . no, he had the same smile.

Their eyes met and Fanny suddenly knew

that he didn't like her. She shivered. It felt odd, such intimate dislike.

'You'd better come inside,' he said. 'We can't talk out here.' He looked around as though someone might be listening to them.

'I'll turn the car first.' She wanted him to have to remark on it. Equally she didn't want to make a mess of reversing such a large vehicle, not in front of him. But when she parked outside in the road and walked with him up to the house, he said nothing.

She followed him through a much-mirrored hall to the sitting-room. Money wasn't his problem, Fanny thought, unless it was having too much of it. The room was huge, all glass windows and regimented settees facing out across a dazzling white terrace round a swimming pool to a shrubbery and more lawn. There wasn't a single familiar thing in it. He hadn't kept anything from the old days with her.

'Did someone die and leave you a fortune?' she asked. 'Or is Tracy one of those advanced American women who pays alimony?'

Man walked across the parquet floor to throw open the patio doors.

'It's awfully stuffy in here,' he said. Like a madman he busily opened all the windows. He stood with the wind ruffling what was left of his curls.

She moved about, touching the furniture. She thought he meant her to admire the room and the lawn and garden now on display through the open windows. Maybe the open windows were meant to show off the clean air of Ruislip.

'Can't you stop fidgeting about and come here,' he said. 'I've got to talk to you.'

'You keep saying that,' she said. 'What's stopping you? I'm listening.' She smiled, but got nothing in return. 'Why do you keep looking out of the window?' she asked.

Fanny, looking past him across the terrace to the shrubbery and the carefully tended lawn, could see nothing. There was the bee-like hum of far-off lawn mowers, but there was something missing.

'Why aren't there any birds singing?' she asked. 'With all those bushes, this should be a great place for birds.'

'Don't ask me,' he said.

Why's he sulking? she thought. It's as though he's set up a surprise party for me and can't get me to walk into the room where everyone is waiting with the cake.

She walked towards him, saying, 'All right, Alan, I'm sorry, I'll be serious. What's the matter? What's worrying you?'

He took her hand. His palm was damp. She wished he'd smile the old smile again. Without it, she had a lot of trouble looking at him. She turned her head away.

Out of the corner of her eye she saw something dark move beyond the terrace. She turned back to Alan.

Something exploded, making such a loud noise Fanny closed her eyes.

When she opened them again she saw Alan dropping as though his bones had melted. There was something awful on his shirt front.

Fanny threw herself on the floor behind one of the over-stuffed armchairs.

She lay tense, afraid to move, waiting.

She did not know how long she lay there. She knew Alan was dead even though when she peered round the edge of the chair all she could see was his feet. They didn't move.

'Alan,' she said.

There was no answer. She reached out and grabbed one of his shoes. He still didn't move. The curtains stirred across the open windows in the breeze. She could smell some kind of sweet flower. And then she heard birds singing again. Whoever had been hiding in the bushes with a gun in his hand had gone.

She got up at last. He was dead all right, there wasn't any doubt about it. She went to the drinks cabinet and swallowed a hefty slug from the first bottle that came to hand.

What do I do now? she asked herself. I should call the police. But what are they going to say, me reporting another body? They're not going to believe anything I tell them. They'll probably think I did it, getting even with the ex.

Alan had been afraid of something, but

what? He'd said he wanted to talk to her about TROD. Did it have something to do with the company?

And then she had a horrible thought. Was it Alan they wanted to kill? She remembered how he'd wanted her to be by the open window, an easy target. And ever since she arrived, he'd been behaving as though he knew there was someone else there. Was it a set-up? Was she the intended target?

She sat down on the far side of the room, away from the body, while she collected her thoughts. Alan was dead, she had to get that into her head. He hadn't run off with Miss America, or left the country, or gone to prison for embezzlement, which was the kind of crime she'd always thought he'd commit. He was dead.

She couldn't make herself feel anything. Her brain was like cotton-wool. I've got to call the police, she told herself.

There was a sudden loud banging on the front door. Fanny felt her heart leap and the blood surge in her ears.

She kept low, creeping along the walls of the sitting-room and down the hall towards the door. She crouched behind it, her eyes on a level with the letter-box. She lifted the flap carefully.

Whoever had been on the step had moved away. She opened the flap a little more.

Then a man walked into view round the side

of the house. He stopped and stood back, looking up at the bedroom windows. Then he turned and walked away into the dark shadows of the macrocarpa trees.

In his hand he carried a small black gun. The man was Gaylord Poyntz.

CHAPTER TWENTY-FIVE

Fanny crumpled on the floor. She felt sick. Gaylord had killed Alan.

It was too horrible. He had followed her up here to spy on her. Then, insanely jealous, he had seen them standing close together at the window and he had killed him. No, Gaylord wasn't jealous, there was something more serious than that. He must be one of them, the bad guys, in on the whole criminal scam, the killing of Mr Burroughs, Sir Stafford's phoney car crash, her own abduction.

She tried to get to her feet but her legs felt like rubber. She sat with her back propped against the door and stared at her repeated reflection in the hall mirrors. Gaylord had always been one step ahead of her. He'd been in the telephone box in Rowfield when she went to report Mr Burroughs' murder. Even if his phone was out of order, why would he need to telephone at that time of night? But he'd walked her home. He couldn't have got back to the cottage and removed Mr Burroughs' body as she talked to the police. Or could he? She'd waited on the bridge for ages after that, before he suddenly popped up saying he'd been waiting for her. He'd have had time then. And he threw away the blood-stained candlestick. He had also undermined her with the police. It was perfectly clear to her now, the way he turned up by magic in Copsey when she rescued Sir Stafford. There were so many things that were suspicious about Gaylord Poyntz. What was he actually doing in Rowfield? He couldn't be doing much of a job on his book of drawings of England simply sitting in the mysterious Harry Hughes's house and taking his dogs for walks. And the mysterious Harry Hughes was suspicious too, the village had always thought so. Of course Gaylord had been some help and he'd put her on to Percy Parfitt. But that was too neat. Why should a cartoonist know who was who in such an obscure area of expertise?

Fanny felt a fool. She had actually let him hold her hand as he led her from one idiotic blunder to another, and all the time she'd taken him for an amiable buffoon. Worse than that, he was a man she was falling in love with. He had been playing with her, but what the game was she didn't know.

She was about to make her way out of the house when she heard someone at the front door.

'If she's shot him she'll be armed,' a man said.

'Sounds like a straight domestic to me,' another man said. 'She's probably in there weeping over the body.'

'Thank God for nosy neighbours, eh, sir?'

'Where would we be without them,' the other man said. 'You take a look round the back. Keep out of sight.'

Fanny heard the sound of feet trying to move quietly on gravel.

Of course, Fanny thought, someone heard the shot. Those men are policemen and they're going to arrest me for murdering Alan.

She had to get out.

She knew she had little time, just while those big-booted policemen went round the back of the house.

There was a back door in the kitchen, and another door leading to the garage. Fanny remembered that Alan had left the garage door open when he took her into the house. There was her way out.

She kept low so that a policeman peering through the window wouldn't be able to see her. It was a nice kitchen, she thought, bright and cheerful. There was a mug on the pine table, and a chair pushed back as though Alan had got up in a hurry. It was L-shaped, and the door to the garage was not visible from the outside. Fanny carefully stood up, pressing against the wall.

She glanced at a cork board on the wall. It was festooned with holiday postcards, an Indian takeaway menu, the business cards of a plumber and a firm of radio taxis. Pinned over a photo of Alan at the helm of a boat, smiling that old smile, was a piece of ruled paper torn from a notebook. She recognized Alan's writing. It read, 'Tuesday 11 p.m. take-off. Cancel milk and papers.'

Today was Tuesday. Alan had been planning to go away. Fanny pulled the piece of paper from the board. The photograph of Alan fell to the floor. She folded the paper and put it in her pocket.

She opened the door to the garage. Alan's silver Mercedes stood there gleaming. I should've taken the keys from his pocket, she thought, but it's too late for that now.

She peered round the garage door. A policemen was standing at the far side of the house. He was turned away from her. Then he went into the bushes peering into a window of the house. She heard the sound of breaking glass. Trust the cops, she thought, breaking in when those huge sitting-room windows were wide open.

She used the cover of the macrocarpa trees to move out into the road where the big Buick was still parked where she'd left it.

There was another car parked on Alan's drive, her own old Renault.

Fanny ducked behind a hedge. She was

short of breath. She had to have time to think. The cops would have checked the licence number. They would know it was her and not Miss America who had been in the house. She wondered if they had checked out the big Yank car as well. Thank God I didn't park it in the drive, she thought. At the side of the road like that, there was nothing to associate it with anyone visiting Alan.

And then for a moment she thought she should go back to the house and tell the cops the truth. It had been a mistake to flee. She hadn't killed Alan, she was innocent. Why should she run away? After all, she didn't have the murder weapon. She'd seen Gaylord with that. They could search the place and not find it. That would prove she couldn't have done it. When they did find it, if they did, it would be far away from the scene of the crime—or still on Gaylord. They couldn't charge her with murder if they didn't have the gun. Or could they? They did some pretty strange things these days. Besides, she'd be locked up while they were finding out that she couldn't have done it, and she wanted to know what was going on. Perhaps Alan's murder had nothing to do with whatever was going on at TROD. But maybe it did. The cops wouldn't know that, though. There was no reason, either, why they should connect this murder with what they'd already filed as a fatal traffic accident.

Fanny left the cover of the hedge and ran

for the Buick.

CHAPTER TWENTY-SIX

Fanny slipped into the driving seat of the Buick and let off the brake so that the car slid quietly down the slope before she started the engine. It was the quietest getaway she could manage.

At the bottom of the close, she looked in the rearview mirror to check that no policeman had run out of Alan's driveway after her. There was no sign of life.

Then a pair of eyes met hers in the mirror.

She opened her mouth to scream but Gaylord put his arm round her neck and clamped a hand firmly over her mouth.

'Shut up, Fanny, it's OK. Everything's going to be all right,' he said in her ear. 'Now let's get out of here before the police catch on.'

He took his hand away from her mouth but remained leaning over her shoulder, looking around. Fanny put her foot on the pedal and the car shot forward.

'Hey,' he said, 'this car needs careful treatment.'

'You bastard,' Fanny said. 'You bloody bastard.'

'What the hell's this?'

'How could you, Gaylord? Not just Alan,

but everything else. Letting me go on, pretending you were helping.'

'I understand you're upset. But calm down. We've got to think clearly. They know it was you, so we haven't much time.'

She was going to curse him some more but then she remembered he had a gun and didn't mind using it. And before he did use it again, she wanted to know what was going on.

'Were you working with Ian Ramsey?' she asked. 'He's got to be involved.'

She felt his weight shift as he sat back in the seat. She glanced in the rearview mirror and saw his face. He looked astounded. And, she thought, worried.

'Fanny, you've got to pull yourself together. Gee, I wish I knew more about criminal psychology. Not criminal, no, no, I'm not calling you a criminal, Fanny. I'm sure you had a good reason. Perhaps it was a cry for help. But the police aren't going to understand that. As far as they're concerned you killed him, ergo you're a murderer.'

She saw his eyes roll in his head.

She stamped on the brake and stopped the car.

'You think *I* killed Alan? Is that what you're saying? The police may think that at the moment because some bastard told them I did, but I can soon clear that up and prove I didn't. It's not my fingerprints on the gun.'

Gaylord began to laugh. 'You think I killed

your husband?'

'Gaylord, it's no use pretending. I saw you. I saw you holding the gun and coming round from the back of the house only a few seconds after it happened.'

'Jesus,' he said, 'what did I ever do to deserve this? Fanny, calm down. Take big breaths. I don't even know how to fire one of these things. Here,' he added, 'you take it.'

He leaned over the seat and dropped the gun into Fanny's lap.'

'You bastard, you think I'll pick it up and then my fingerprints will be on it. Well, if I do pick it up, it'll be to kill you. I mean it.'

Gaylord opened the car window and leaned back against the back seat. There was a short silence. Fanny drove on. She didn't know what else to do. She concentrated hard on the road ahead. Her eyes were brimming with tears and she could scarcely see. She wiped them with the back of her hand.

'You've set me up,' she said. 'First you put the police against me, making out I'm a mad drunk, and now you've got them thinking I murdered Alan.'

'Look,' he said at last, 'I was worried about you. I didn't trust your ex-husband. Remember you spelled out the address over the telephone; I even got to thinking you might've done that as subconscious insurance. Fanny, I parked your car in the drive. Would I have done that to set you up? Yes, I would, of course. That's exactly what I'd do if I were the killer bent on framing you. So forget that part.'

In the rearview mirror she saw him smile, but then he got serious again.

'I got to the house, I saw the Buick. I knew you were there. I heard a bang so I went round the back thinking you and he might be slugging it out in the garden. The revolver or whatever it is—that thing—was lying on the grass. I picked it up. I thought at first it was a toy. Then I got to the terrace and I saw . . . well, you know what I saw. There was no sign of you. I admit, I jumped to a certain conclusion.'

'You thought I'd killed him?'

'Of course I did. And then I thought you must've got away without me seeing you, so I came to check that the car was still there.'

'And then you called the cops, I suppose?'

'When I saw them coming I got into the car and laid low. If *I'd* done the killing, do you think I'd have waited around with them there?'

'You could have, out of morbid curiosity.' But she was beginning to believe that he might not have shot Alan.

But somebody had, Alan had the hole in his chest to prove it.

Gaylord sat in the back seat rambling on. He was trying to make her feel better, she supposed. Every now and then he shouted that she was going too fast.

He didn't look like a killer, but somebody was, and maybe they didn't look like it either.

The cops had been on the scene awfully quickly. She had assumed some nosy neighbour had heard the shot and called them, but there was some distance between one house and another in that well-heeled close.

There was something else, too. When she came out of the house and into the road something had been missing. She hadn't seen any of those nosy neighbours looking to see what was going on.

No, it wasn't a resident of the close who had called the police. It was someone else. The cops had been tipped off. But by whom?

There was a mysterious game being played here, and ever since the night of the disappearing corpse she had been in the middle of it, with other people pulling the strings. She had to start doing some string-pulling of her own.

She drew into a layby beside a telephone box.

'You could phone from a pub,' Gaylord said. 'I could use a drink.'

'I can't wander around in public,' she said. 'The police think I killed Alan, remember.' She leaned over to open the glove compartment and took out her handbag.

She found a handkerchief in her bag and wrapped it round the revolver before putting it in her pocket.

'I'm only giving you the benefit of the doubt,' she said, taking the ignition key with her.

In the telephone box she fumbled in her bag and found her contacts book. How would she have listed it? C for Campaigns? P for Protests. Desperately her eyes followed the Ps and then she had it. Why on earth Political? she thought. Religious would be nearer the mark. She lifted the receiver and started to dial.

The number rang and rang. Then a non-committal voice said 'Yes?'

Fanny left her message and put the phone down. There was no time for questions.

'You know,' Gaylord said through the open window as she went back to the car, 'this is all getting really serious. I mean, very, *very* heavy. People don't get shot dead with guns. Not at least people you know.'

His face was pale. What had happened seemed at last to be sinking in. He had never seen Mr Burroughs lying dead on her sitting-room floor, he hadn't been locked up in that foul house in Copsey. Until now he'd probably been thinking of it as a game, Fanny thought, even the car chase and her driving into the river and the fight in the pub probably didn't seem too sinister to him.

But what about me? she asked herself, wasn't I thinking of it the same way? Even Mr Burroughs' body seemed like a hoax.

'You sure it wasn't a heart attack?' Gaylord asked. 'Those young executive high-fliers drop dead of them.'

'He had a hole in him,' Fanny said. 'Now shut up and let me think.'

There was a link in all this, but she just couldn't see it.

Then she looked down and what she saw made her shudder.

CHAPTER TWENTY-SEVEN

There was dried blood on her legs, and on her skirt. She began to shake. For a moment she thought she was going to faint and then she felt sick.

'What's wrong?' Gaylord asked.

He had moved into the front seat. He followed her eyes.

'Gosh,' he said.

'I didn't notice it before,' Fanny said. 'Oh my God!'

She thought she could feel the blood now, wet and sticky, but that was her imagination. It was dry by now.

'I think I'm going to throw up,' she said.

'Me too,' Gaylord said. 'I suppose a drink is out of the question.'

'I can't drive. Look.'

She held out her hands. They seemed to have a life of their own. She kept hearing the loud explosion and seeing Alan drop to the floor. 'It's hitting me now,' she said, 'the shock.' She couldn't stop her teeth chattering.

'I'll drive,' Gaylord said.

He got out and came round to the driver's side. Fanny felt her legs wouldn't carry her round the car. She was glad of the Buick's bench front seat. She slid over.

'Is it on my face?'

Gaylord got behind the wheel. He leaned forward and examined her. 'It's not so bad,' he said. 'You're imagining it, like Lady Macbeth.'

Fanny wasn't listening. She felt like screaming. This must be hysteria, she thought, but she'd never felt it before, not even when she found out about Miss America.

'I've got to change these clothes,' she said.

'You'll have to stop and buy something.'

Gaylord was calm, driving the big car smoothly along the tree-lined road. He said, 'With your car in the drive where I left it, they'll think you're still hiding in the house. Only after they've searched the place thoroughly will they realize you've somehow left the neighbourhood. The police aren't looking for me or Harry's car. Not yet at least. Please God we can keep it that way.'

Fanny kept taking deep breaths. It wasn't a choice, she had to, or she felt she'd suffocate. Her head seemed to be full of fizzy water.

'What's next?' Gaylord asked.

'I don't know.' She shook her head in confusion. 'I don't know. It sounds crazy, but I think Alan was setting it up for me to be killed. Then something went wrong and he was shot instead.'

'There's nothing that doesn't sound crazy about this business,' Gaylord said. 'Alan must've known this Ian Ramsey quite well to be able to get you the job.'

'He was certainly making money somewhere, with that big house and a new Mercedes,' Fanny said.

'That wasn't the lifestyle he'd accustomed you to when you were married?'

'You're joking! We never had a penny. Then things got a bit better. I was never quite sure why they did, and before I had time to ask he was off with Miss America.'

'Pity you didn't have time to ask. Whatever it is, they think it's worth killing old men and ex-husbands for.'

'There's only one lead, and that could be nothing. He'd left a note on his message board. I brought it with me.' She found the note in her pocket and smoothed it out. 'Look, "Tuesday take-off 11 p.m." They could be pulling out. Sir Stafford said that his unexpected return to the office would force their hand. This could be it.'

'How's that help? We don't know where they're going to.'

'We might know where they're going from.'

'Do we?'

'Sure, Copsey. There's that old American

airbase there and you found out that planes were using it again. Mysterious planes landing and taking off at night, wasn't that right?'

'It's a long shot.'

'It's all we've got.'

'Copsey, then. If there's nothing going on, you can hide out in that charming little holiday cottage you looked over the other day.'

'I can hide out? What about you?'

'Me? I wouldn't be seen dead in a place like that. I don't need to hide out, remember, I'm not the one the police are after.'

Fanny saw movement on the road ahead.

'What's that?'

'What's what?'

'That? What's that?' She pointed.

'Cops,' Gaylord said. 'They must think there's a killer on the loose.'

He slowed down. Ahead a police car partially blocked the road. Two policemen stood beside it, waving them down.

Fanny pulled the revolver out of her pocket and dropped it on the floor. She kicked it under the seat.

'My skirt,' she said. 'I'm covered in blood. They'll be certain to see.'

Gaylord got a map out of the glove compartment. 'Use this,' he said. Fanny spread it across her lap.

'It's a map of the United States,' she said.

'We'll tell them you're lost.'

Gaylord opened the window and leaned out.

The policemen looked grim.

'Hi, boys!' Gaylord said. 'Broken down, have you?'

One of the policemen stepped forward. He was very young. He looked affronted.

'This is an official roadblock,' he said. 'Would you mind identifying yourself.'

Gaylord produced a driving licence.

'That's all I've got on me today,' he said. 'We left our passports at the hotel, didn't we, hon?'

Fanny broadened a smile into a grimace. She hoped that was what young policemen thought American women looked like.

'Hey, what's going on?' Gaylord asked.

The young policeman dropped his official severity. 'There's been a shooting near here.'

'Say,' Gaylord said, as though impressed. 'Did you hear that, hon? Here we are in old England on our honeymoon without the kids and there's a shooting. We might as well have stayed in New York.'

Fanny kept smiling. Her jaws hurt. She wondered how American women stood it.

'New York!' the young policeman said, 'that's a place I'd like to visit. I've been to Florida, but I'd like to go to New York next time. I don't suppose you know the 84th precinct?'

Gaylord laughed. 'Funny you should mention that. I saw Ed McBain walking up Fifth Avenue once. That was a day! I wonder what old Ed would make of your shooting here?'

'Oh, it's a domestic, almost sure to be,' the young policeman said. 'We're on the lookout for the ex-wife.'

'Really?' Gaylord said, bending forward with interest. 'What happened? Was he late with the alimony cheque? What's she like? We might see her. We could let you know.'

'I wouldn't advise you to approach this lady, sir. According to our computer she's liable to do anything. Mental problems, I believe, an alcoholic.'

'Sad,' Gaylord said. 'A sad case.'

The policeman stepped back, admiring the bulky lines of the old Buick. 'Is this a hired car, sir?'

'This? No, no, it's mine. You can check that out. Name's Poyntz, Gaylord Poyntz. I bought this over here. I saw it and I couldn't resist it. I guess I must be one of the few Americans to come to England to buy an American car. I guess you'd call that crazy.'

The young policeman didn't seem interested in Ed McBain and American cars any more. He was looking at Fanny. She tried to keep smiling but she couldn't.

'Where are you going now?' he asked.

'The Randolph Hotel in Oxford,' Gaylord said.

The policeman leaned into the car. His eyes went to the map on Fanny's knees. Or was it the map he was looking at? She was sure now that he was looking at the splattered blood on her legs.

There was the patter of an approaching police motorcycle on the road behind them. The policeman stepped back from Gaylord's car.

'Oxford's up ahead, sir. Won't take you long.'

'Have a nice day!' Gaylord said with a breezy wave. They moved slowly past the police car, then he accelerated away.

'My God,' Gaylord said, 'when he stuck his head in the car.'

'I've got to get out of these clothes,' Fanny said.

'You can't go into a shop all covered in blood.'

'No, but you can.'

'Me? I don't even know your size.'

'I'll tell you. Just get anything.'

'I'll be embarrassed.'

'Not as embarrassed as I am covered in my ex-husband's blood.'

'You've got a point there,' Gaylord said.

They were coming to a small town.

'Stop,' Fanny said suddenly. 'There's a shop. Go in there. I'm a size 12. Or maybe a 14, depending on the make.'

She sat in the car watching the tall figure amble to the shop as if he didn't have a care in the world. Through the glass she could see him inside making movements with his hands to a saleswoman, outlining the shape of the woman he was buying clothes for. The salesgirl laughed. Then Fanny thought she'd better keep her eyes open for policemen.

When he got back to the car he was carrying a large carrier bag.

'This is the best I could do,' he said.

'Anything will do,' Fanny said, but then she looked inside the bag. 'What the hell is this?'

There was a minute skirt in studded leather, and something in red satin.

'I didn't know what to say. I got kind of carried away.'

'Did you say I was going to a costume party? And fishnet stockings?'

'What's wrong?' Gaylord asked. 'Don't they go with your shoes?'

With much wiggling she got on the leather skirt, the minute halter top and the fishnet stockings. Whatever she looked like, it was better than her bloodstained clothes.

'I look like a B-picture gun moll and they're looking for a gun moll.'

'No they're not. They're looking for Sir Stafford Williams's highly respectable public relations lady and a distraught ex-wife who's neurotic enough to plug the ex-husband. That's two different other people from the way you look now.'

'You're a master of disguise, Holmes.'

'You bet.' He looked at her legs. 'Gee,' he

said, 'those fishnet stockings look peculiar. Sexy, but peculiar.'

'Not as peculiar as they feel. Anyway, they beat the hell out of bloodstains.'

But after a time she forgot about the fancy dress. She even began to think that Gaylord had bought it on purpose to take her mind off Alan dropping dead in front of her, and the police being after her for his murder. But a ballgown and a diamond tiara wouldn't have taken the weight of that off her mind.

She had to face that she wasn't in this situation by accident. Somebody had planned everything, and every move she'd made had been in accordance with that unknown plotter's plan. But now she was making decisions for herself. At the old airfield in Copsey she hoped to find out who was pulling the strings.

What she'd do then she didn't know. But no matter what happened, Gaylord had made certain she was all dressed up for the part.

She fumbled for the gun and handed it to Gaylord. 'You'd better take this,' she said.

He put it in his pocket.

CHAPTER TWENTY-EIGHT

It was a windy night. The full moon was cloaked in racing cloud. There was still a pinkish glow in the sky where a spectacular sunset had gradually faded behind the black silhouette of the hangars and old sheds.

'Come on,' Fanny said.

'Come on where?' Gaylord asked. 'I thought we were going to watch and report. We've sat here bang up against the perimeter fence for hours watching nothing happen. I was going to suggest we go for a drink.'

'You know I can't go in a pub, I'm a wanted woman. It's getting dark, we should get into position.'

'What are *you* going to do?' Gaylord asked.

'*We* are going to climb over the fence, of course. It's not difficult.'

She got out of the car and came round to the driver's door to open it and pull him out.

'Listen,' he said, 'I don't mind helping you escape from the scene of a murder, but I don't want to get *really* involved.'

They walked up to the fence. It was ancient. It sagged when Fanny pulled on it.

'Watch out what you're doing,' Gaylord said, 'that's private property.'

'We'll climb over here,' Fanny said.

'You think I'm going to climb that?'

'Don't be so feeble. You're thirty-eight, not eighty-three.'

'I'm not climbing that fence.'

Fanny took a deep breath and jumped up to grab on to the wire as high as she could, jabbing with the toes of her shoes for a foothold.

'You could get paid real money in Vegas for an act like that in those stockings,' Gaylord whispered from below her. 'Twice nightly.'

Gradually Fanny worked her way up the link chain. It was rusty. She could feel the rust on her hands.

'I suppose I really shouldn't be looking at this,' Gaylord said.

'At what?'

'At the view from here.'

The hard part was rolling over the top to swing down the other side. Old barbed wire was woven through the top and caught her clothes. For a moment she was held there helpless, the wire hooked to her blouse.

The cheap material tore. Fanny fell heavily, landing on her back on the grass with a loud gasp as the breath was knocked out of her.

'I don't suppose you could do that again in slow motion?' Gaylord asked out of the shadows.

'Certainly not.'

'Amazing,' he said.

Fanny sat up. She was unhurt. 'OK, now you.'

'Climb that fence in this suit? Hang on a minute.'

There was a silence. She heard the car door open. He's going to sit there in comfort till I come back, she thought.

'Gaylord!' she called.

'OK, OK, I'm here. But I won't forgive you for this, and I might as well tell you that if it was daylight and there was any chance at all of someone seeing me doing this, I wouldn't even try.'

He threw something over the top of the fence, covering the barbed wire at the top.

'What are you doing?'

'That's the car rug. I'm not risking this perfectly good suit. Listen, if I should die, kindly do not go into details about the ignominious nature of my fatal accident.'

The wire slumped under his weight and he was able to jump from the top to the ground beside Fanny.

'I don't know why you had to make such a production of that,' he said. 'Say, you look terrific by moonlight with that torn blouse. And when you were climbing the fence in those fishnet stockings . . .'

'Come on,' Fanny said. 'And shut up. These people are murderers.'

'You think I've forgotten that? For one single second?'

'You'd better give me the gun.'

'The gun? Oh, that gun. I haven't got it. It must've fallen out of my pocket.'

He went on his hands and knees patting the grass round the fence for the gun.

'I suppose the loss of the gun is a tremendous disaster,' he said, still on his hands and knees. 'Without the gun I'll have to overpower people with my bare hands. Or maybe I could use hypnotism. This scene is incredible. I can't believe I'm down here in this wet grass actually looking for a gun in case I have to shoot someone. Correction. In case you have to shoot someone.'

'Keep your voice down,' Fanny said, 'we don't know who's around here.'

'What a date this is turning out to be. My friends won't believe what you English girls get up to. They think you're all still in twin sets and pearls sipping Earl Grey tea.'

'This is no time for jokes, Gaylord.'

'You don't think so? Listen, if I've ever been in a situation where a few laughs were vitally necessary, this is it.'

He couldn't find the gun.

'We'll have to do without it,' Fanny said.

She moved as quickly as she could across the grass towards the buildings in the middle of the airfield. She had to bend almost double against the wind. Gaylord, muttering to himself, followed.

When the bright moon sailed out from the speeding clouds it was quite light. Fanny hoped that if there was a look-out, the line of houses behind them would mask their silhouettes. Otherwise, anyone glancing across the field could surely see Gaylord trying to keep down but jumping like a huge bull-frog as he went.

They reached the first shed. She could hear Gaylord panting beside her.

'Stop breathing like that,' she whispered.

'I can't not breathe,' he said. 'Breathing, I mean it's—'

She grabbed his arm and pulled him in close against the wall.

'Fanny, what was that phone call you made?' Gaylord asked. 'It was to the police, right?'

'No,' Fanny said, 'it wasn't to the police.'

'A social call?'

It wasn't, but Fanny didn't say. Everything, she thought, might depend on that phone call and she didn't want to tempt fate by talking about it.

'I just wanted to tell you again before I forget,' Gaylord said, 'you've got great legs. Climbing that fence! One day I'll put a big wire fence in the bedroom. You know, for when I'm older and greyer and need reminding.'

'You're babbling because you're nervous,' she said.

'No kidding? Is that what it is? I suppose this is an everyday occurrence for you, seeing your ex-husband shot down and lying dead on the floor like a draught excluder inside the patio doors and then—'

'You wait here,' Fanny said.

She ran forward along the side of the hangar. At the end of it, she peered round. There was another shed ahead and, using this as cover, she ran towards the centre of the group of buildings.

Rounding the end of the shed she stopped short.

The building opened on to what had once been a concrete apron for the landing strip. On this, against the light coming from the open-fronted hangar, she could see the outline of an aircraft. It was a twin-engined prop plane. Lights flicked inside it where the cargo doors gaped open. There was a fuel tender parked under the wing.

Two men appeared out of the plane and stood on the ramp of the open cargo hold.

Fanny moved back into deeper shadow. She remembered Alan's note. 'Take-off 11 p.m.' The villains were making a run for it. Whatever it was that would explain the deaths of Mr Burroughs and Alan must be in that plane. Somehow she had to stop it taking off.

A hand grasped her shoulder and she nearly cried out.

'It's me,' Gaylord said, 'the strangler. Don't scream.'

'Do you want to get us killed?' she whispered. 'Look!' She pushed him forward to peek round the edge of the shed.

In an instant he was back behind her. Now his voice was as low as hers.

'What do you think they're doing?'

Fanny crept forward for another look. She could see the two men carrying something between them. Lanterns moving inside the open gates of the shed suggested more men there.

'Gaylord, will you do what I want for once?'

'Fanny, this is not the time or the place.'

'Do it, do you hear? Go back along the side of this building, and when you get to the back, bang on the corrugated iron as loudly as you can.'

'Bang on the wall? But they'll hear me!'

'That's the idea. You'll have to bang really loudly or they'll think it's just the wind.'

She heard him muttering as he moved away. 'Be careful,' she whispered. 'Don't do anything rash.'

She waited for the sound of Gaylord banging on the metal. It seemed a long time. She had no very clear idea of what she was going to do, just that somehow she must delay the plane's departure. She thought, thank God there was someone there when I called; if it had been an answering machine they mightn't check it for days.

'Where is he?' she said under her breath. 'What's he doing? Don't tell me the idiot's broken his ankle or something.'

When it did come the battering on the corrugated iron startled her. It was followed by a bloodcurdling cry straight out of a cowboys and Indians movie.

The lights went out in the hangar and inside the cargo hold of the plane. A lantern on the apron lurched, and then Fanny could see men running round the opposite side of the building.

She ran to the aircraft. The refuelling hose was still attached to the tender parked under the wing. Fanny had to climb on its fender to reach up. There was a clip holding the nozzle of the hose in place. She unhooked it and the hose snaked across the tarmac spurting fuel. If enough of it spilled it might delay them taking off.

She jumped off the tender, landing in a puddle of fuel. She could feel it cold inside her shoes.

'Must've been kids,' a voice said from the direction of the shed. Fanny recognized the voice. It was the Millwall supporter.

'Little bastards. Smells like the fuel line's come loose,' another voice said. That's George Miller, Fanny said to herself. The lights went on again. A group of men came out of the shed. Fanny took a step away from the plane towards them. She stood silhouetted against the subdued glow inside the cargo hold and they saw her.

'It's that flash bint again,' the Millwall supporter said. 'How'd she get here? She's supposed to be locked up on a murder charge, ain't she?'

'We'll finish her off this time,' Miller said.

They moved towards her. She ran for the cover of the sheds, throwing herself on the ground against a wall. She looked back at the scene round the aircraft. They hadn't even bothered to follow her. A man picked up the fuel hose and reattached the nozzle to the plane.

It's going to be too late, Fanny thought, perhaps the dozy cow who answered the phone didn't pass on the message.

Keeping low and outside the range of the lights around the plane, Fanny made a run for the hangar where the men were working.

Moving along the wall, she found a place where a rusted corrugated iron sheet had worked loose and been folded back in the high wind. She climbed through. She was inside the hangar, behind the area where the men were working.

A number of crates were stacked there. Fanny crouched behind them, and tried to decide what to do next.

She was suddenly aware that she was not alone. There was someone moving close by. She shifted position and peered round.

Against the light from the front of the hangar she could see the outline of a man pressed against the side of a crate.

They know I'm here, she said to herself, there'll be others. They're trying to trap me.

And then the man moved towards the open area at the front of the hangar, and she saw him clearly silhouetted against the light.

She'd know that shape anywhere, the stocky outline, the broad shoulders and shortish legs. It was Ian Ramsey.

He wasn't stalking her. He was examining the crates. Checking the loot, she thought, while he waited for the plane to be ready. And then he'll be off and he'll have got away with killing Mr Burroughs and Alan. The police won't believe my story. They'll think the plane was a figment of my imagination like Mr Burroughs' body. I'll have no evidence against anyone, and I'll be done for Alan's murder.

Fanny followed Ramsey between the crates, hoping he wouldn't turn round. At one point she tripped over a pile of wood. Someone had opened a crate and forgotten to nail all the slats back. Ramsey stopped and looked back. She held her breath. He can't see me, she told herself, he's looking out of the light into the darkness. But she held her breath until he turned away.

She picked up one of the loose slats and followed him.

She must stop him before he got too close to the lights where the Millwall supporter and Miller and the rest of them were working.

She raised the weapon and ran forward to bring it down on the back of his head.

But he heard her, and turned. The blow caught him a glancing knock above the ear. She saw the look of amazement on his face as he raised his arm to ward off a second blow.

And then she was on him, trying to hit him again, but she was afraid of making too much noise. Luckily he didn't shout out for his men to come to help him. He'd probably be embarrassed not being able to overpower a woman, Fanny thought.

He wasn't as weak as he looked. He knocked the slat out of her hand. Again she felt like turning and running away. But she mustn't do that. This man and what was on the plane was the evidence that would clear her.

She dived at him. She felt her weight was feeble when she collided with his bulk, but she caught him off balance and he went down. She straddled him.

The fight seemed to go out of him. She saw a coil of rope, very old and greasy, almost within reach. With her knees pinning his arms down she tried to reach the rope.

'You've got this all wrong,' Ramsey said. He was deliberately keeping his voice down.

She leaned over, reaching for the rope.

'Here,' a voice said behind her.

Fanny went rigid with fear. But the voice was a woman's, and it was familiar.

Holding Ramsey's arms down with her knees, her hand clamped over his mouth, Fanny turned her head.

Behind her stood the incongruous figure of Miss Field. She was wearing her familiar ill-fitting tweeds and one of her shiny blouses with its outsized bow. Fanny thought she looked marvellous. 'Miss Field!' she said, 'am I glad to see you.'

CHAPTER TWENTY-NINE

Miss Field gave no sign of being glad to see Fanny. She was frowning at Ian Ramsey.

'Tie him up,' Miss Field said. 'We'll deal with him later.' She pushed the coil of filthy rope towards Fanny with the toe of a court shoe.

'It was him,' Fanny said, 'it was Ian Ramsey, I *knew* it was him.' Fanny was babbling with relief. 'I can hardly believe you did all this yourself too, discovering his racket like this.'

Fanny took the rope.

'Don't do it,' Ramsey said.

'Keep quiet,' Fanny told him.

'You don't understand,' Ramsey said. His face was covered with sweat. In the pale light he looked sick. He'll be sicker when the police get here, she thought.

'You've no idea how grateful I am, Miss Field,' Fanny said. 'I was at a complete loss on my own. The police think I've shot my ex-husband.'

She had to sit Ramsey up to put the rope round him. She was still shaking from the fight and the effort of looping the rope round him made her breathless. She wiped her face with the back of her hand. Her hands were covered with grease from the fuel hose. She knew it must have come off on her face. She smiled at

Miss Field, but Miss Field didn't smile back.

'It's not me,' Ramsey whispered.

Fanny had him tied securely now.

She stood up, looking down at her blouse which had been even more torn than before in the struggle. The ridiculously short leather skirt had twisted round, and the fishnet stockings were ripped. She smiled again at Miss Field and all at once she knew what a fool she'd been. Even without the look on Miss Field's face Fanny knew what the story was.

Of course it had been Miss Field all along. She was the only one who knew Fanny was going to see Alan. And before that it was she who'd ordered the special taxi to take Fanny to Copsey. And the letter from Sir Stafford, they only had Miss Field's word that it was genuine. Any secretary with Miss Field's time on the job could forge the boss's writing.

But why? Why had she done it? What had turned a fluffy old maid like Miss Field into a killer?

It flashed into Fanny's mind that she could overpower the old woman. But Miss Field was ahead of her. Before Fanny could act Miss Field called, 'Miller! And you, Jones. Over here!'

George Miller and the Millwall supporter appeared. Their shadows loomed against the hangar wall. The men were motionless but their shadows had a life of their own as the flickering of the lights made them move.

'What d'you want done with them?' the Millwall supporter asked.

'Tie her up,' Miss Field said, and suddenly she didn't look old or feeble. 'I'll keep an eye on her. Make sure she did a good job tying Ramsey up and then take him away. I don't want them getting together to plan any last minute surprises now. Really,' Miss Field said to Fanny, sounding like her old nervous secretary self, 'I just don't know what to do with you.' Her tone of voice in the bizarre setting made her seem mad.

'Miss Field, what made you do this?' Fanny asked.

'What was I supposed to do?' Miss Field said, sounding as if she were talking of a minor incident in the office. 'All those years being treated like a lower form of life. It's perfectly all right for Sir Stafford, and many others I could name, to make fortunes out of these foreign countries, but when someone like me takes advantage of a situation, then people start to disapprove.'

If it was the mother and the old aunt that had driven Miss Field to such extremes Fanny thought she should get her talking about them to gain time, but the Millwall supporter said, 'We got to stop this mouthy bint and the bloke for good.'

'Yes,' Miss Field said, 'yes, I know.' She dragged out the words as though she was deep in thought. 'We'll take them with us and drop them out once we're out over the open sea, that'll get rid of the evidence once and for all. And hurry, we're running out of time.'

'What?' Fanny said. She couldn't believe she had heard correctly.

Miller and the Millwall supporter also seemed in doubt.

'Out of the plane, you mean?' Miller asked.

'Of course out of the plane,' Miss Field said, and the voice she said it in, as if she were talking about using the best china for an important client's tea, made it all the more scary.

The Millwall supporter turned and looked at Fanny. 'Seems like a waste,' he said. 'And it's extra weight taking off in this wind.'

Fanny could feel her mouth go dry. She'd never been afraid of flying or of heights, but now she was. I've got to stall them, she thought, but when she opened her mouth to speak no words came out.

'Are you a pilot?' Miss Field said.

'No,' he said.

'Well shut up, then.'

'It was the pilot said we'll have trouble taking off in a gale with our load,' the Millwall supporter said. 'They could tip the balance.'

'Not for long,' said Miss Field.

'Miss Field,' Ramsey said, 'there's no need for this. I won't say anything. Why should I? I don't care. I only came because I was curious.'

Miss Field turned away and started to check

one of the packing cases as though she had nothing to do with it now.

'Do you understand what's going to happen?' Ramsey said to Fanny. 'They're going to take us up in that plane and throw us out.' His face was pouring with sweat. Fanny didn't feel any too good herself but she didn't know what to say, and she couldn't do anything. She tried to kick Miller but he held her legs down. She felt the rough rope being wound tightly round her ankles.

'Tie her legs good,' Miller muttered to the Millwall supporter. 'She's the kind of bitch who likes to kick.'

'There's not enough rope to do a good job on her arms,' the Millwall supporter said.

Miller pulled a length of fraying binder twine out of his pocket.

'Put this round her wrists. Put her hands behind her back. She won't get out of that.'

The Millwall supporter did as he was told. Then he propped Fanny against the case next to the one Miss Field was checking.

'She's all yours,' he said to Miss Field. Miss Field did not turn round. Fanny looked at her back and it was as though she had never seen her before. She must've been playing a part all those years at TROD, Fanny said to herself, pretending to be a nervous Nellie. Or perhaps it was a life of crime, with hulking great men to boss about, that had brought out the outlaw in Miss Field, the Clapham spinster. Either way, it made no difference, Miss Field was now a dangerous enemy.

The men pulled Ramsey out of Fanny's sight. She heard a stifled grunt and then one of the men laughed. She could imagine the kind of temptation Ramsey, trussed up and helpless, would be to natural born muggers like Miller and the Millwall supporter. And they hadn't exactly restrained themselves with her. She was becoming increasingly aware of how tightly they had tied the twine round her wrists. She gritted her teeth at the pain of it biting into her flesh.

Miss Field had her back turned, leaning over the cases.

'What's in them?' Fanny asked.

'Tinned food, mostly,' Miss Field said.

'Why are you unloading them here?' Fanny asked. 'There's no shortage of that kind of thing in the supermarket.' It's grotesque, she thought, it's as though we're having a conversation about the weather in the office.

'No, of course not,' Miss Field said. 'These are part of the aid we send out. The TROD people think it's aid, but we exchange it for what I call our investment capital. We've had to take the stuff off to make room for our people.'

'You mean you're making a run for it?'

'Yes. You got too close, Mrs Dinmont. I know you didn't realize what you were getting involved in, but you've made it difficult for us.'

She might be talking to a girl from the typing pool about a mistake in the filing, Fanny thought.

'But Miss Field, what's going to happen to your mother and your aunt?'

Miss Field turned to look at Fanny now. She smiled pityingly.

'My mother's been dead for years, and I have no aunts that I'm on speaking terms with.'

Fanny knew she must look amazed because Miss Field shook her head at how easy she had been to dupe.

'I needed cover for taking time off, and as excuse if I seemed agitated and upset. I was agitated and upset, I'm not a criminal, you know.'

Fanny wondered just what she would call dumping people out of planes but she didn't ask.

'In case you were wondering, Miss Field,' Fanny said, and she tried to echo Miss Field's tone, 'I've got the icon. The one poor Mr Burroughs hid.'

'Where did he hide it?' Miss Field asked. She stepped back from the packing case and faced Fanny. 'Those two morons said they looked everywhere.'

'I've got a small collection of icons,' Fanny said, 'they're in my spare room at the cottage. They're copies, or nineteenth century, nothing valuable. But Mr Burroughs left it there, and your men didn't know the difference.'

'I'd a buyer for that one,' Miss Field said. 'Pity. But I suppose you've put it out of harm's way?'

'Yes,' Fanny said. It's very rare.'

'Of course it is,' Miss Field said. 'Some of the priests have been copying the rare icons for display in the churches and smuggling the real ones out for convertible currency.'

Miss Field smiled. She looks very pleased, Fanny thought, she's proud of herself.

Fanny wasn't going to congratulate her. 'And all done under the guise of aid flights?' she asked.

'No one loses.' Miss Field seemed offended at some implied criticism. 'The company supplies the aid anyway.'

Miss Field moved on to another case and began to check its contents.

As soon as Miss Field was turned away, Fanny began to work her wrists against the twine. The pain brought tears to her eyes, but she could feel a strand give. Still, she couldn't stop herself grimacing with pain. If Miss Field saw her face, she would know at once what she was doing.

'So the art treasures are your personal sideline?' Fanny said, as though she were making polite conversation. Another strand gave.

'It wasn't difficult to arrange,' Miss Field said. She still had her back turned as she checked the cases. 'I only used what was there for the taking. Nobody else thought of it, that's all.'

'But Mr Burroughs was killed,' Fanny said. 'Sir Stafford was abducted. And Alan was killed. He had something to do with this, didn't he?' Fanny could hear her voice sounding peculiar with the pain of the twine digging into her wrists. She hoped Miss Field would put it down to fear at the thought of being tossed out of the plane somewhere high over the sea, and if Miss Field thought that, she wouldn't be far wrong. Fanny knew she was bleeding, the blood was making the twine slippery, but she continued to work at it. Miss Field might turn round at any moment.

The frayed binder-twine gave. Her wrists were free.

Miss Field did not answer Fanny's question. She continued to check the contents of the case. She pushed it aside quite easily and dragged up another. When I get free, Fanny thought, *if* I get free, I'm going to have a fight on my hands with her.

'Why is what I'd like to know, Miss Field?' Fanny asked. 'Why did you do it if it wasn't for your mother and aunt?'

Miss Field turned and looked down at Fanny. With her giant shadow looming behind her, Fanny felt like a child watching a cartoon monster.

'It wasn't like that, I never planned it out

like that. At first it was a way of making a lot of money without hurting anyone. I liked it, it was exciting. I'd never known anything like that.'

'But it isn't a game, Miss Field, not any more.'

Miss Field turned back to the crate. She doesn't want to face the truth, Fanny told herself.

'You may not have killed Mr Burroughs or Alan with your own hands,' Fanny said, 'but you're going to throw me and Mr Ramsey out of the plane, you're going to kill us. That's not the same thing as stealing art treasures and exploiting people, is it?'

Fanny did not think Miss Field was going to answer. At last, though, Miss Field said slowly, 'It doesn't mean anything to me. You and Mr Ramsey are in the way, and this is a simple way of putting you out of the way. Like Mr Burroughs and Mr Dinmont.'

'How did someone like you . . . how did you get involved with people like Miller and the other man?'

'Jones? They were working for Mr Dinmont. And Mr Burroughs wasn't meant to die. He made a run for it, and Miller got carried away.'

Her back remained turned and Fanny used her freed hands to lever herself into a more upright position against the case.

'And what made Miller get carried away

when Alan was shot?'

'That was your fault, I'm afraid. You were really getting in the way. The plan was to dispose of you in what one might call a domestic setting. By the time they found your body, Mr Dinmont would have been on the flight to South America with us tonight. But when it came to setting you up, Mr Dinmont's heart wasn't in it. I suppose he was sentimental. I couldn't take the risk. So Miller disposed of him and left you to talk your way out of a murder charge if you could. Mr Dinmont should never have got you the job at TROD. If I hadn't been off work at the time it would never have happened.'

Fanny eased her arms forward and began to explore the knots in the rope round her ankles.

'Why did he?' she asked.

'Sir Stafford suddenly came up with this notion about a public relations department. No one else wanted it, but he wouldn't be put off. So Mr Dinmont suggested you because if Sir Stafford employed you, he'd be able to pull the strings. That was the expression he used.'

Fanny felt sick. She could hear Alan saying it. He probably believed it, too.

Miss Field was still speaking in that formal secretary voice of hers, politely giving the men their titles. 'So Mr Dinmont mentioned you to Mr Ramsey. He and Mr Ramsey were friends, or at least they played golf together. It was a useful cover for him to call at the office when

Mr Dinmont and I needed to talk. Mr Ramsey didn't suspect anything.'

Miss Field opened another packing case.

Is it true? Fanny asked herself. Would I have done as I was told? If I hadn't found Mr Burroughs' body? Or met Gaylord? Oddly enough, meeting Gaylord changed a lot of things.

'What about Sir Stafford?' Fanny asked. 'Why did you have to abduct him?'

'When Mr Burroughs started asking questions there were a few decisions to be made so I could wind the operation up quickly. Sir Stafford would have found out what was going on.'

Fanny started to work on the cord knotted round her ankles. One knot began to loosen.

'So you could do what you liked with the company and everyone believed Sir Stafford was making the decisions?'

'Certainly, I hadn't been Sir Stafford's secretary for twenty years without learning how to forge his handwriting.'

She's so pleased with herself, Fanny thought, and a good thing too, she's not noticing what I'm doing.

'Of course I didn't want a great hue and cry looking for Sir Stafford. That's why Miller and Mr Dinmont staged the car crash. It gave me what I needed. I could do anything I wanted by pretending he had given me instructions.'

'Alan? You mean Alan was involved in

killing Mr Burroughs?'

One end of the cord was free.

'Mr Dinmont had a key to your cottage. He helped George Miller hide the body there, and then remove it. I must say, Mrs Dinmont, I'm surprised you hadn't changed the locks when Mr Dinmont left you.'

Fanny finished untying her ankles. She got to her feet as quietly as she could, hoping Miss Field wouldn't turn round before she got a good head start making a run for the nearest telephone to call the cops.

But there was a crash from somewhere in the hangar behind them and Miss Field jumped and turned round and saw Fanny was free.

Fanny closed her fist and pounded Miss Field on the jaw.

Miss Field fell down in a sitting position. She looked surprised. She put a hand to her face.

'You little cat,' Miss Field said, 'I should have known that was the sort of behaviour I could expect from you.'

She started to get to her feet but Fanny said, 'Don't get up, Miss Field.'

'You'll ruin everything.' Miss Field remained on the floor.

Fanny thought she had better hit her again to keep her quiet while she made a run for it. But she couldn't do it. Miss Field was back to looking like the dithering faithful old secretary with an unwell mother and aunt in Clapham.

Fanny reached down and ripped the bow off Miss Field's blouse and stuffed it in her mouth. Then she looped the dirty old rope round her feet and hands.

Fanny began to edge her way to the front of the hangar when there was a shout. Miller and the Millwall supporter came out of the plane. They were carrying iron bars and they looked mighty excited about something.

Fanny pressed against the wall. She was sure they hadn't seen her. They were angry about something else.

At last, Fanny thought, she didn't let me down.

CHAPTER THIRTY

'Now!' yelled a female voice from the hangar door. Fanny made out a flurry of dark figures rushing into the hangar. In the dim light they looked outlandish, horribly threatening in dark clothes with balaclavas pulled down over their faces.

'Melanie!' Fanny shouted. She had to shout again to make herself heard above the wind. 'I'm over here. I thought you weren't coming.'

Then the leader pulled the balaclava off her head.

'This is the scum we're after, right?'

Melanie Musgrove asked. 'Where are the monkeys?'

Two of her balaclava-wearing supporters pushed a man forward. They were holding on to him so he couldn't run away. It was Gaylord, looking wind blown.

'Fanny,' he called, 'what's going on? I told them there were no monkeys in crates in here, but they didn't believe me.'

'Oh Gaylord,' Fanny said, 'thank God people don't believe you! They'd have gone home to bed if they had.'

'Actually, if it wasn't for him we'd never have found you,' Melanie said. 'We were lost. He brought us here.'

Gaylord, who had been looking rather guilty, brightened. Only now, with Melanie's animal rights women in control of the hangar, did he seem to realize that Fanny had arranged to have them here when she made the telephone call on the way from Ruislip.

'What about the plane?' Melanie said. 'Are the monkeys in the plane?'

'There aren't any monkeys. I'm sorry, Melanie, but I lied to you when I rang you because I knew I was going to need backup and I couldn't go to the police. You were the only person I know who could get people to come out for something like this. This is a good cause, I promise, even if it's not about animals.'

For a moment Fanny thought Melanie and

her supporters might attack her.

She gave Fanny a withering look. 'I don't know what you think you're doing,' Melanie said, 'but if that plane isn't carrying a consignment of poor little monkeys being imported for animal experiments, what is going on? And whatever you've got yourself mixed up in, Fanny, I think I'd better warn you, the police are on their way. I wasn't going to let a publicity opportunity like this pass.'

Melanie looked at Fanny and was about to say something more when there was a tremendous din of police sirens. The plane and the mouth of the shed were bathed in light. A policeman was shouting something incomprehensible through a loud hailer.

In the commotion Miss Field appeared, unbound and looking perfectly like her normal self except for her blouse where the bow had been torn off. She walked up to Fanny as if she wanted a friendly chat.

But before Fanny could say anything to her she saw Inspector Fulwell coming into the hangar, followed by Sergeant Kerslake. Inspector Fulwell walked slowly across the tarmac to Fanny. He had a superior smile and seemed about to speak, but he was interrupted by much shouting. A group of policemen were loading Miller and the Millwall supporter into a van. Miller shouted at Miss Field, 'I'll make you pay for this. I'm not taking all the blame for killing that geezer, you old bitch.'

Miss Field turned as if annoyed by a minor distraction. She smiled at Inspector Fulwell. 'That's the only kind of language his type knows, I'm afraid,' she said.

Inspector Fulwell smiled at her. 'Don't worry, ma'am,' he said, 'we'll soon have this cleared up and you can go home.'

'That would be nice,' she said.

Inspector Fulwell took Miss Field's arm, obviously he thought of her as an old lady who might have brittle bones or suffer from dizziness.

'Maybe I can find you a cup of tea,' he said to her.

'You know she's your villain, don't you?' Fanny said. 'She's Sir Stafford Williams's secretary and she's the one who had Mr Burroughs killed and Sir Stafford abducted and my husband shot. And she was going to take me and Ian Ramsey up in that plane and push us out over the sea.'

Inspector Fulwell's superior smile returned.

'Another of your stories,' he said, 'like the runaway corpse?'

Fanny was about to ask Inspector Fulwell how he could be so stupid when there was another commotion. Ian Ramsey appeared accompanied by a policeman. Ramsey was moving stiffly and rubbing his wrists. There was blood on his shirt. Miller and the Millwall supporter had obviously kicked him about.

'We found him tied up under the plane,' the

policeman said. 'He says he doesn't need an ambulance.'

'Will somebody please explain what's going on here?' Inspector Fulwell said. Sergeant Kerslake pulled out a note-book and took the top off his ballpoint pen.

'I'm trying to tell you,' Fanny said. 'This woman . . .'

'Will somebody *apart* from Mrs Dinmont please tell me what's going on here,' Inspector Fulwell said.

'Fanny knows the truth,' Ramsey said. His voice croaked as though it hurt him to speak. 'She discovered what was going on.' He turned to look at Miss Field and shook his head in bewilderment. 'I don't understand what came over you,' he said.

'I'm not ashamed of what I did,' Miss Field said. 'I'm only concerned about how Sir Stafford is going to cope without me.'

'That woman is going to make life hell for everyone in Holloway Prison for a few years to come,' Gaylord said.

'All right, Mrs Dinmont, you win,' Inspector Fulwell said. '*You* tell me what's going on.'

'I take it that you're prepared to listen to what I say and not call me a liar, a drunk and a raving lunatic?' Fanny said.

Inspector Fulwell did his best to smile. 'I may have been misled,' he said. 'But I'm listening now. So, from the beginning . . .'

'It's a long story,' Fanny said.

With a flourish, Gaylord produced a hip flask. 'Then I think we could all do with a drink.'

'Tea all round, Kerslake,' Inspector Fulwell said.

We hope you have enjoyed this Large Print book. Other Chivers Press or Thorndike Press Large Print books are available at your library or directly from the publishers.

For more information about current and forthcoming titles, please call or write, without obligation, to:

Chivers Large Print
published by BBC Audiobooks Ltd
St James House, The Square
Lower Bristol Road
Bath BA2 3BH
UK
email: bbcaudiobooks@bbc.co.uk
www.bbcaudiobooks.co.uk

OR

Thorndike Press
295 Kennedy Memorial Drive
Waterville
Maine 04901
USA
www.gale.com/thorndike
www.gale.com/wheeler

All our Large Print titles are designed for easy reading, and all our books are made to last.

WEXFORD PUBLIC LIBRARIES